REVENGE AT POWDER RIVER

Sam Heggarty returns home to hunt for the gunmen who robbed and executed his father. As he makes his way back, he witnesses another murder and stumbles across a clue to the people responsible for his father's death. He discovers that the one person who may hold the key to the identity of his father's murderers is someone that everyone else is intent on killing. Heggarty will have to save the life of a man involved in his father's death …

JOHN McNALLY

REVENGE AT POWDER RIVER

Complete and Unabridged

LINFORD
Leicester

First published in Great Britain in 2018 by
Robert Hale
an imprint of The Crowood Press
Wiltshire

First Linford Edition
published 2021
by arrangement with The Crowood Press
Wiltshire

A catalogue record for this book is available
from the British Library.

ISBN 978–1–4448–4669–0

3 4 1 4 6 6 0 1

Published by
Ulverscroft Limited
Anstey, Leicestershire

Printed and bound in Great Britain by
TJ Books Ltd., Padstow, Cornwall

This book is printed on acid-free paper

1

The man behind Walter Heggarty grabbed him and pinned his arms back, twisting them like rope. The big man, Stanton, stood in front of him and drove his fist as hard as he could into his guts. His stomach buckled, they all heard the impact and the air go out of his lungs. He slumped forward as his breath caught in the back of his throat.

The big man's face had no expression, his eyes looked black and glazed with light from the lamp. He had a large head, a neck as thick as a tree stump, fists that were square and rough and covered in hair like tangled wire.

'Sign it.'

'Never,' said Heggarty, gasping, a pulse jumping in his throat. 'You'll have to kill me first. Go to hell.'

'I've been in hell all my life, mister and got to like it,' said Stanton and hit him six more times, clubbing blows to

Heggarty's body and arms. When they let him go, he sank to the floor and lay like a crumpled coat.

They walked away from him and Stanton said to a third man sat at the table, 'Jarrett, take his money and those bits and pieces, and put them in your bag with the papers and get out of the way. I'm going to lay him out on the table and butcher him until he begs us to let him sign.'

Behind them Heggarty staggered to his feet, lurched over to the fireplace and pulled a loaded short-barrelled shotgun off the wall. His hands tingled and his arms felt like lead as he fumbled with the trigger but he managed to snap one hammer back as he turned. Stanton stood in front of him with his arm outstretched, pointing his gun at Heggarty's chest with his eyes fixed on his face. Stanton smiled as he squeezed the trigger and the room exploded with smoke and noise, and the air was bitter with the smell of gunpowder as the gun bucked in his hand.

The shot took Heggarty in the chest

and he died where he stood. The little man Jarrett jumped up from the table and ran out of the door with the bag.

Stanton's eyes were empty of emotion. He slid the handgun back into his rig and said, 'Marcello, check he's dead.'

Marcello looked down at the gaping wound in the man's chest.

'He's dead as a door nail, I reckon.' Marcello was a heavy man with a backside like a wheelbarrow full of mud; he breathed loudly through his mouth and had eyes that were no more than slits in his fat face. 'I don't think you should have killed him. What are we going to do now?'

'It's simple,' said Stanton. 'The Colonel told us to clear the land for him around the east of Powder River. So we drive the sodbusters off and he gets the land. That's what we've been doing these past six months, ain't it? You come along so they see that it's no good complaining to the law because you and your tin badge are stood next to me when I give them hell. This one was different because he was too mule-headed to move and he's held out to the last. We needed him to sign his land across but he wouldn't. He sent his wife away because he thought he was smart. He had his chance, he pointed a gun at me and now he's dead.'

Marcello said, 'But won't the Colonel be mad now that you've killed him?'

Stanton shook his head. 'No, he just wants us to get it done, he don't want to know how we did it or excuses for why we didn't. He don't do things to people, he just makes them happen. How dumb are you, Marcello? The Colonel keeps his nose out of this. That's why the land clearing is our job. The murder's on us.' He pointed at Marcello and his voice hardened. 'That's us I said, not just me. You with me on that?'

'But we ain't got the land.'

'No, we ain't but when the wife comes back, I put a gun against her head and we force her to sign the land over. Job done.'

'What about that attorney, Jarrett, he's

4

just run out on us.'

'What about that attorney Jarrett, he's just run out on us,' mimicked Stanton. 'Jarrett did the paperwork on the land deals, that's his job. He's run out on us and that means we cain't trust him anymore. He witnessed the killing and he's the only one that can link us to what just happened. I'm going to find him and kill him. Is there any of that you don't get?'

He leaned forward, grabbed Marcello by the throat and shook him until his eyes almost rattled in their sockets.

Stanton was a brutal man, ask anyone. He'd like as grin before he hit you. He was brought up on the Wyoming border down Lonetree way. His father worked the land, hardscrabble with no give in it. His mother died when he was eight, it seemed like she'd just had enough of the work and suffering and quit on life. His father, a hard drinking man, despised his wife for escaping and took his anger out on the young Stanton. He beat him with a strap and worked him like a mule from dawn until dusk for the next eight long years. And then one day Stanton snapped. He was working in the field, he carried the heavy plough strap and mule harness across his shoulder and pushed the plough through the hard crust of shallow flinty ground. He followed the mule as they struggled in the furrowed ground under the blazing sun. Heat waves rippled off the hardpan and dust devils spun in the wind. He saw his pa stagger across the rutted land, his eyes dull with drink.

'Boy,' he called, 'you ain't nowhere near finished, you lazy, gutless runt.' He held a wide leather belt in his hand and he lashed down, the buckle caught Stanton high on the head and raked down across his cheek.

Stanton fell over and his old man stepped in and kicked him in the head, breaking his nose and splattering blood across his face. Stanton surged to his feet as anger and frustration welled up in his chest; his eyes locked on his father's face and stayed there. For the first time in his sixteen years of life, he saw fear cross his father's face. His father realized, too late, that his snot-nosed son had grown into a man, he licked his lips and they felt as dry as sand and he smelt his own fear in the heat and dust of the land.

Stanton stood over six feet tall, his shoulders and arms ridged with muscle and filled with rage and resentment. He swung a huge fist that thundered into the side of his father's head and almost ripped his face off. Then he stepped up close into his father's shadow and stared him down. Stanton's eyes looked like you could scratch a match on the eyeballs and he wouldn't even blink. Stanton's father raised an arm in fear to protect his head and shoulder and he fell to his knees. Stanton grabbed a long scythe from the mule's harness, gripped the oak shaft with both hands and swung it in a wide arc and the sleek honed blade buried itself in his father's chest.

Stanton unharnessed the mule and

rode away. He never looked back and he never went back. He never regretted it, either.

Now here he was, ten years on and twenty dead later, killing for a living. He reckoned they all deserved what they got. He took his misery out on everyone else. Stanton still held Marcello by the throat and he fought the impulse to snap his neck there and then but he knew he still needed him. He let go of Marcello's shirt and tried to relax. He looked under the table and as he straightened back up he said, 'Not only has the durned lawyer Jarrett run out on us, he's taken the bag with the papers, Heggarty's money and bits of jewellery. Still, it makes the killing look like a robbery gone wrong. That's what you tell folk, someone killed and robbed Walt Heggarty. Let's get out of here and wait for the wife to turn up and then we force her to sign over the land. Meantime we find your friend Jarrett and I kill him.'

A couple of days later, the dead man's

son, Sam Heggarty, made his way across Wyoming, determined to find his father's killers.

2

Sam Heggarty sat in the hotel room. The wind and rain thumped like a fist on the wooden walls and the window.

He sat and stared at the planked floor for a long time as if he might find the answers there. He blew out his breath, grabbed his bag, threw it onto the bed and opened it up. He lifted the bundle wrapped in a burlap sack and felt the familiar heavy weight of the gun rig and two hand guns. He promised his wife when their first son was born four years ago that he had put them away forever. She saw him take them out of the drawer yesterday and watched him stow them in his bag before he set off, but she hadn't said anything. She knew they had been a gift from his father when he joined the army. She understood why he took them as he set off to find the men who had killed his father. She accepted what he had to do; that was what made him the man he was.

He missed his boys already, his breath caught in the back of his throat but he pushed those thoughts aside.

He had a job to do and there was no quitting in him at all.

The guns were oiled and their surfaces had a dull sheen in the soft lamp light. He picked one up and opened a fresh box of cartridges. He released the loading gate, pulled the hammer back, rotated the cylinder, clicked the chambers through one at a time and thumbed six rounds in. Then he did the same with the second gun. He filled the thirty-two cartridge loops on the calfskin belt.

He stood and rolled a cigarette, dragged a match across the wooden post of the door frame and his face flared in the cupped flame of the match under the brim of his hat. He was in his mid twenties, pools of colour high on his cheeks and dark eyes webbed with tiny lines at the corners. He lit the roll-up and inhaled the smoke deep into his chest. He balanced the cigarette on the old dresser by the wall while he pulled on his boots then pushed one gun down the waistband of his pants and went downstairs for a drink.

The saloon throbbed with noise.

Through the slatted swing doors, the wide boardwalk flanked the dusty street, with hitching posts and a water trough. Inside, a long polished oak panelled bar ran the width of the room. Around the base of the bar was a dull brass foot rail with a row of spittoons spaced along the floor. Along the ledge, towels hung for the drinkers to wipe the beer suds from their moustaches. Someone thumped out a tune on an old piano in a corner but no-one listened. The tune became lost in the sounds layered across each other — raucous voices lit with drink, card players oblivious to their surroundings called and slapped cards on the table, boots and chairs scraped on the rough wooden planking as the drifters, thieves, cowboys and town folk drank and gambled their way into another tomorrow.

'A beer,' Heggarty called as he eased his way to the crowded bar. The bartender nodded and started to draw the beer.

'I'm next, boy,' said a slurred voice.

Heggarty half turned and saw a spiteful face red with a whiskey flush glaring at him, the eyes vague and empty.

'There's no problem, friend,' said the barman. 'It don't matter none, I'll serve you as well.'

The drunk's face looked as still and blank as a flat wall, his breath foul with cheap drink and tobacco. He reached a big calloused hand across and emptied out half of the beer that the barman placed in front of Heggarty. The liquid pooled on the bar and sloshed down over both men's pants.

The drunk said, 'Now look what you've gone and done, you goddamn clumsy fool. I'll hit you 'til your teeth rattle like dice in a cup.'

Heggarty turned to his right to get a proper look at the troublemaker. He saw a man with narrow shoulders, wide hips and a lump of fat rolled around his middle. He had a thick blond moustache and a face the colour of fresh sunburn, his open jacket showed his rumpled shirt dark with sweat rings under the arms. Heggarty said, 'You're getting on my wrong side right quick, mister. That drink's on you.'

The drunk blew out his cheeks, sucked in air and as he straightened up, his hand went for his gun. He drew but as it cleared the holster, Heggarty's left hand snaked out and chopped down hard on the man's gun hand. The drunk's face jumped with pain and shock and his Colt clattered to the floor. Heggarty's right hand jabbed out and his fist hit the gunman over his heart and he watched the drunk grunt and fall to his knees. Heggarty kicked the gun on the floor and it skittered across the boards and disappeared under a nearby table.

He watched the man on his knees for a moment, saw him struggle to breathe, his face crimson with pain and anger as he fought for air.

Heggarty turned away. An old timer, a scrawny old type all sinew and gristle leaning on the bar, winked at Heggarty. He lit a pipe and watched Heggarty through the smoke as it drifted across his face. He liked the look of the young man, smartly dressed in a charcoal cor- duroy shirt, the sleeves rolled up on his sunburned arms, his slim body as com- pact and hard as a pile of bricks. He was fairly tall with a fresh, honest face, short dark hair and long sideburns.

Heggarty slid the half empty beer glass across to the old timer and said, 'Have that one on me, partner.' He walked off and as he passed in close, he whispered, 'Holler if he tries anything,' and he left the bar without looking back. His right hand rested on the gun tucked down the waistband at the front of his pants. He felt the cold weight in his hand, the familiar grip comforted him as he headed back to his room.

3

Early next morning, the stagecoach pulled up in front of the hotel. It had a four horse team, a driver and an armed guard. They aimed to cover seventy miles that day. As they stopped, the driver jammed on the brake with his foot and the stage rocked on the two leather strap thorough braces that supported the coach. The guard laid his shotgun in the front box and climbed down from his seat on the left of the driver and crossed into the hotel. He was a cheerful, pot-bellied middle-aged man, freshly shaved but his skin had baked in the sun over so many years it looked like old wrinkled leather. He walked through the open doors, bringing with him the smell of the early heat from the street and stale tobacco.

He glanced over at the clerk behind the desk, nodded and said, 'Fine morning, we've got three passengers to pick up.' The clerk adjusted the glasses on his nose and looked around.

Heggarty sat in a wooden chair against the far wall, he pushed his hat back on his head, sat up and half raised his hand to show his ticket.

A small man wearing a dark baggy suit and black felt derby hat that looked too big for him stood leaning over a table, looking at the *Oregon Herald* spread out in front of him. He held out a ticket without looking up.

A chunky figure stepped out of a door from the saloon and waved a ticket.

'I'm Sorensen,' he said in a thick phlegmy voice, his eyes puffy and his face pale, as white and tight as paper.

Heggarty recognized the voice, looked up and saw the drunk from the fight in the bar the previous night. He did not say anything, he figured it was all over between them but watched the man as he moved into the light. Sorensen's glance flicked across to Heggarty for a second but he lowered his eyes and walked past to stand by the door.

The guard cleared his throat.

'The stage is going from Moneta through Powder River to Chugwater in Platte County. We'll arrive the day after tomorrow. We have one passenger for Powder River, so we'll be stopping there a spell before we move on to Chugwater.' He paused, his voice sounded heavy and tired. 'Even if you've travelled with the Cheyenne and Black Hills Stage Line before, I'll remind you of the most important company rules before we start out.' He glanced at Sorensen 'There's supposed to be no drinking liquor, but if you must then pass the bottle round. We've no ladies travelling so you can smoke and use rough language, it don't matter none to me. But don't snore right loud or use anyone else as a damn pillow, it always leads to trouble.'

He looked at each passenger and said, 'You boys keep your guns with you but don't fire out of the windows at the animals, it scares the horses something shocking. I figure there's no grief between any of you, let's keep it like that.'

18

Heggarty looked over at Sorensen but saw his gaze fixed on the floor in front of him. Sorensen leaned his head back, rolled his neck and said, 'Can we get gone?'

'We surely can, yes, sir, the last rule is we don't keep the stage waiting.'

Sorensen got on board first. Heggarty threw his bag up to the guard who shuffled it across the coach roof and lashed it to the rails then, holding his rifle, Heggarty climbed on board. The small man followed, he folded his newspaper, slipped it into his jacket pocket and pressed it down flat.

'No luggage,' he said, looking up at the guard and smiling.

Inside, the small man, Farrington, sat by the door and Heggarty sat opposite him with his back to the horses. He slid across the seat a little to give Farrington more leg room and Farrington nodded his thanks and they settled for the ride.

Sorensen sat by the far door facing the horses, his feet on the seat opposite and he lay slumped on the bench with his hat pulled down over his face and slept, or pretended to.

'I'm Sam Heggarty. Going far?' said Heggarty, smiling at the little man. He liked the look of him, he was in his early twenties, small with a clear open face and curly hair.

'My name's Farrington. I'm off at the first stop, Powder River, how about you?' His voice surprised Heggarty, it was deep and raspy like someone cutting lumber with an old saw.

'Next one down the line after you, Chugwater,' said Heggarty.

Farrington studied the other passenger Sorensen's faded red shirt, crumpled and threadbare tan canvas trousers and his hat with a tall crown and thick sweat stains around the headband. Farrington looked him up and down, turned to face Heggarty and raised his eyebrows and smiled as the driver shouted, 'Next stop is the swing station in six hours, give or take.' The stage jolted as he released the brake.

The stage surged forward as the driver

urged the horses on, snapping the reins over the back of the team. The coach groaned and swayed as they gathered speed and moved out of town. As they left the buildings behind, the horses picked up their pace and moved along the rutted trail, their drumming hoofs and the iron-rimmed wheels throwing trail dust up in a cloud that snaked out behind them.

'I don't expect anything much will happen this trip, do you?' said Heggarty.

'You never know,' said Farrington.

★ ★ ★

Down the trail a piece, the attorney Jarrett rode his buggy and cursed his luck. He wished he hadn't seen Stanton kill Walt Heggarty. He thought about how things kept on going from bad to worse. He didn't go looking for trouble but it usually found him. Well, he reflected, he made some poor decisions back in Boston, that was true. Using clients' money to buy some sure fire investments seemed

21

a good idea. Of course, he'd have paid them back out of the profits. Then it all went belly up and he had to get out. But Godforsaken Wyoming, that was another step down to hell all right. The Colonel was an impressive man with a simple scheme to buy the land in and around the Chugwater Valley and sell it at a big profit. He didn't know how the Colonel knew about his little problem in Boston but he didn't seem to care and let him manage the paperwork. Mind you, he said he'd kill him if he did anything wrong.

And Stanton had put a knot in one or two heads along the way to get folk off the land but that seemed reasonable business, it was only a few sodbusters after all. But that murder was way out of line. Stanton was out of control. That idiot Marcello was a stupid, fawning yes man. He had a ten dollar Stetson on a five cent head.

Yes, he ran when Stanton killed Walt Heggarty, well, any civilized person would do the same thing faced with cold blooded murder. And yes, he took the bag but after all, it was his paperwork inside it. The money as well, he reasoned, well, he'd earned that. A thousand or so in cash looked fair for the work he'd put in. The cheap costume jewellery was worthless, he needed to dump that really.

He hid for a couple of days until his trail cooled, it was uncomfortable but he figured Stanton would be looking for him and he needed to clear the territory and start over. Jarrett knew with certainty that Stanton would kill him now because he knew too much and witnessed the murder. Stanton terrified him, he never smiled and never talked about his personal life, if he had one. He just looked at you like you were something on the end of a dung fork and crushed everyone who got in his way. For sure, he was in a heap of trouble now Stanton was looking for him.

Jarrett jolted out of his daydream as the buggy tipped sideways and he rolled out into the hot dust. He stood and, to his horror, he saw two Indians walk up out of a draw and run towards him.

★ ★ ★

The stage with Heggarty on board made good time until in the afternoon it slowed and they heard the driver shout to his guard over the thrum of the horses' hoofs. Heggarty and Farrington looked at each other, lifted the leather curtains and poked their heads out of the windows. The breeze tugged at their hats as they squinted through the choking dust cloud.

'What's happening?' shouted Farrington, ducking back inside and brushing the dirt from his face with the palm of his hand. Before Heggarty could reply, they heard the unmistakable crack of two gunshots and the wagon jerked as the driver hauled on the brake and shouted over his shoulder to them.

'There's a buggy part blocking the trail, looks like it's sand locked and there's a body by the wheel.'

Heggarty picked his rifle up from the floor under his seat and Farrington drew his hand gun, both men relaxed and calm as they checked their weapons.

The horses blew and stomped as the stage settled, the metal axles clicking in the heat. Heggarty and Farrington climbed out. In front of them, the ground fell away into the distance where the trail twisted like a rutted ribbon until it disappeared in the heat haze that shimmered on the horizon.

Slewed across the trail a hundred paces or so ahead was a little buggy with a small dun horse standing in the traces with its head down, it trembled from its withers to the crop. The tongue of the buggy had twisted, one wheel sunk in the soft sand and grit, tilting the buggy awkwardly.

A body lay next to the half buried wheel and a tubby man stood a couple of paces away with a short barrelled carbine held at his hip. He glanced across at the stage and hurried around the back of the buggy, searching in the trail dust.

The driver stood up in his box, shielded his eyes and said, 'There's a couple of horses in that dip behind that bush over yonder.' He pointed away to the right and Heggarty ran across in a half crouch. The guard and Farrington began to walk over to the buggy. Heggarty reached the bush and slowed as he walked over the rim of land; with his rifle at his shoulder he looked down the barrel for trouble. He saw two ponies looking back at him, their eyes wide with fear.

An Indian lay by one of the pony's feet with his body covered in dirt. His long hair was powdered with dust and his left leg coated in blood and sand that glittered in the sunlight. The Indian pushed himself up with his arms and looked up over his shoulder at Heggarty who stood silhouetted on the hill, his shadow stretching down into the gully.

He noticed that the Indian was unarmed, so he lowered his rifle and walked down to help him.

'He shoots my brother,' the Indian

said in slow broken American.

'Do not move,' said Heggarty. He knelt by the Indian and touched his blood soaked leg. The Indian's face flushed with pain, his skin as taut as parchment but he made no sound. Heggarty could see that a bullet went across the calf, leaving a deep red gouge layered with blood and dirt.

Heggarty crossed to one of the ponies and unhooked a water skin, splashed the water across the gashed leg, washed it clean and tied his bandanna in a tight strap around the wound as best he could. Heggarty lifted him to his feet, supported him with his shoulder and walked him out of the hollow and back to the main trail.

The buggy driver still crouched at the back of the buggy, searching the dusty floor and pushing papers into his bag. The stage guard leaned over the dead body that lay in the heat and dust. The body looked like a pile of sticks and rags with a gun wound in the chest still leaking blood, the smell hung in the air around them.

Farrington watched the buggy driver gather up the spilled contents of the bag and shove them back inside it. The driver sensed someone watching him and glanced over his shoulder. He clicked the bag shut and stood dusting the legs of his trousers and stared back at Farrington with open hostility. Farrington saw the money as the man hurried to close the bag and as their eyes met, Farrington winked and turned away.

The buggy driver noticed the Indian and fumbled for his Colt.

'Don't draw that gun, mister,' Heggarty said in a calm level voice and he raised his rifle one-handed and pointed it at Jarrett's belly.

'They tried to rob me,' shouted the man. 'I should finish him off.' He cocked the Colt but held it down at the side of his leg. Heggarty looked at him and waited.

'Put the gun away,' said Farrington in his gravelly voice, 'before you go get yourself proper hurt.'

They studied the buggy driver. He was

maybe forty, he wore a lumpy suit, had a flabby gut that sagged and bulged like a cushion and a fat chin that rolled in folds over his collar. He stood wracked with indecision, his chubby face slick and oily with fear.

The stage guard said, 'Look, let's all calm down.' He pointed to the buggy driver. 'You, tell us what the hell's going on.'

The buggy driver sighed and said, 'My name is Buford Jarrett, I'm an attorney. I was trying to dig the wheel out when these two damn Indians,' he motioned with his head to the body, 'tried to jump me. I shot him and clipped the other when he ran.' His voice was high with emotion but he looked at Heggarty and stuck his gun back into the holster.

Heggarty glanced down at the dead man sprawled in the dust by the wheel and said, 'It looks more like he was digging the wheel out to me when you took him down. Look at that hole by the wheel, and his hands and arms are covered in dirt.'

The wounded Indian next to Heggarty nodded and held his own hands out, they were thick with dirt.

They all studied the buggy driver, Jarrett, his suit and small derby hat were dusted from riding the trail but his gloves were clean enough.

'That one,' said Jarrett, nodding at the wounded Indian, 'started rooting through my bag.' He held the carpet bag in his hand and pulled it towards himself, hugging it to his chest.

'Kill the Indian and let's get out of here,' said a voice behind them. Sorensen stood unnoticed at the back. 'The only good Indian is a dead one.'

The guard said, 'Hold your horses. These are Shoshone, they're no trouble usually, we should be real careful until we know what happened.'

Sorensen laughed and spat. 'I'd believe Jarrett here before I listened to any goddamn Indian.'

Heggarty waved his rifle at Sorensen and said, 'You need to shut up and get back to sleep. Both these Shoshone only have knives and they're still in their belts. They left their bows back there with their horses, I've seen them. We need to report this and see what their story is. I'm going to take this feller to the next station,' he pointed with his chin at the Shoshone next to him, 'and get them to call in the local town marshal.'

'Right, you do that,' called the stage-coach driver from the trail. 'We're an hour from the next station, we need to get the stage in now anyway. Let's move.'

As they all started to walk, the buggy driver Jarrett said, 'I'm not going with you, I'm heading the other way.'

'Well, you're walking,' said the guard, shaking his head. 'The axle's busted and this buggy ain't going nowhere. Look for yourself.'

Heggarty said, 'You're staying with us anyway until we sort out what happened.'

Jarrett lowered his eyes and without speaking, stalked off towards the stage behind Sorensen. The guard started to loosen the buggy horse from the traces.

'I'll fasten this to the boot of the stage, come on, let's move.'

Heggarty half carried the wounded Indian over to the shade running down the side of the buggy and set him down.

'What's your name?' Heggarty said to the Indian. 'Ahiga.'

'Listen, Ahiga, I'm Heggarty. I'm going to get your ponies and we'll take them and your brother to the next station, do you understand?'

'Yes, I understand.' He nodded.

Heggarty started to move off around the back of the buggy when a glint of gold caught his eye from the dusty ground. He bent down and picked up a small brooch, he rubbed it clean with his thumb and blew the sand off. He stared at the brooch, a small flower inlaid with red glass. His mouth tightened in a grim line as he recognized the brooch but he swallowed his anger. He slipped the piece into his trousers pocket and turned and looked hard at the stage. He knew the brooch belonged to his mother and that it was stolen on the night they killed his father. His blood was singing in his ears but he calmed himself and decided not to rush things, he remembered that the hunter needs time and patience for a sure kill.

He ran for the ponies, led them back and tied them to the boot next to the horse from the buggy. He brought the wounded Shoshone Ahiga up, but as he opened the stage door Sorensen called out.

'That devil ain't riding in this coach.'

'Damn right he ain't,' piped in Jarrett. 'There's no place for that sort of savage in here.'

'For God's sake, get a move on, put him on his pony or something,' called the driver.

Heggarty shrugged. 'I'll ride the other pony but the body's going on top, no argument.' He dragged out one of the buffalo sleeping blankets 'I'll wrap him in this.'

'I'll help you,' said Farrington. They rolled him in the blanket and the guard tied him to the stage roof. The driver pulled off the brake and eased the stage past the stricken buggy then he stood in his box and uncoiled his whip. He held a ten-foot buckskin lash with a hickory shaft, he whirled it with a flourish and cracked the air above the horses and the stage shuddered forward, the three horses with Heggarty and Ahiga tied on behind.

Inside the coach, the drunk Sorensen sat with his usual sour expression, the buggy driver Jarrett nursed his bag and the little man Farrington looked out at the gathering night lost in thought until, finally, he decided that the risk was worth taking.

★   ★   ★

Later, single stars appeared glittering in a grey sky as sunset pushed in on the horizon. The heat and light faded as the horses pounded and the stage thrummed across the hard packed trail, the lengthening shadows deep purple in the gathering dusk.

The stage topped a rise and the driver blew his small brass bugle to alert the station they were almost there. They slowed and rumbled down the hot ground. The home station lay below them in a hollow darkened by the twilight. They pulled up in front of a low single-storey adobe building with a shingle roof, a fenced corral with a large stone water tank and stables running down one side.

The stage stopped with a creak of wood and leather and the stable hand ran from the shadows to see to the team. The horses snickered at the smell of water, their steaming backs haloed in a glittering cloud of the dust swirling around them. The station keeper, a dull looking man with a big chin, short black hair with a lot of grey and a body as thin as a whip watched them in and then walked over to the driver.

'Trouble?'

'Some,' said the driver and he explained about the buggy while they watched Heggarty help the wounded Indian off his pony. The station manager and the driver strolled over to them.

'I'm Mason, station manager,' he said, nodding at Heggarty and the Indian. 'I'm sorry about your brother,' he said directly to Ahiga. 'I've seen him before,' Mason said to the others. 'They're decent folk round these parts and no trouble. Some Shoshone come down off the reservation hunting and the like. We don't pay them no mind.'

He spoke to Ahiga in Shoshoni and listened while Ahiga told his side of the story.

Mason said, 'He says they were out hunting, saw the buggy stuck in the sand right enough and tried to help. They started to dig it out and the bag fell off the back but the driver went plumb crazy, shot his brother and hit him as he ran away. I believe him.'

'I knew it,' said Heggarty. 'I figured something like that, I reckon most of us did. It needs reporting to the nearest lawman. It's goddamn murder and should be dealt with properly.'

Mason smiled and raised his eyebrows.

'You think?' he said. 'Listen, Ahiga just wants to take his brother and get gone. He's probably right. It's still a white man's law in these parts. Most folk around here don't give two nothings about what happens to an Indian, you know it. Probably best to let it go. I'll get the body and the ponies to the stable and see that his leg's tended to.'

Heggarty waited outside smoking a cigarette, he turned as he heard footsteps and the manager Mason stood looking at him and said, 'Forget it.'

Heggarty flicked his cigarette onto the floor and ground it out with the sole of his boot and said, 'I guess I can see it's safer for Ahiga to accept it. I suppose he could be charged with attempted robbery or such like and some would always believe the worst of an Indian. But I don't like it, it doesn't feel right.' He fingered the brooch in his trousers pocket. 'Me and the buggy driver Jarrett have unfinished business anyways … but it can wait.'

Behind them they heard hoofs hammering across the dry prairie and they both turned and saw Ahiga leading the other pony with his brother's body tied across its back.

'He'll deal with it in his own way,' said Mason. 'The food smells good,' said Heggarty.

'It smells better than it tastes, I reckon,' said Mason with a smile. 'Come on and eat.'

They spent the night at the station. After the meal of chilli beef, rice and tomatoes, they settled themselves on the station's hard packed floor rolled in the buffalo blankets and slept.

Jarrett, the attorney, twisted and turned all night, worrying about how he was going to get away.

Farrington and Heggarty both dozed through the night. Listening to Jarrett's restless scuffling in the dark, they were both determined that he would not leave their sight the next day. Farrington thought about the money and Heggarty clutched his mother's brooch and wondered how Jarrett got hold of it.

4

While the stage sheltered for the night, two riders pulled into Moneta and stopped in front of the same hotel and saloon that the stagecoach started off from that morning. The last of the heat still parched the earth, the air smelled hot and the wooden buildings were still warm to the touch. The first rider, the older man, dismounted and the dry leather of his saddle creaked as he stepped onto the street. He lifted his hat and wiped his forehead with his coat sleeve, letting the breeze cool his damp hair.

'I'll get us a room; Harland, you check the horses in at the livery. Ask if they've seen anything that might help us while you're at it.'

He knocked the worst of the dust off his clothes and walked, with a heavy limp, into the hotel reception. The desk clerk watched the man hobble across the hallway, he moved with a stiffness that made him look like he was carved out of wood. He was tall and lean with a full brush moustache and dark hair peppered with grey, a dark woollen jacket and a low-crowned grey hat. Although he was about fifty, with his bad leg and grey stubble he felt and looked a lot older.

'A room for two for the night.' He opened his jacket and showed his star to the clerk. 'I'm County Sheriff Lewis Leeming out of Owl Creek, Hot Springs County. I'm with my deputy, Harland Baker.' The clerk nodded without showing any real interest and swivelled the register with his fingertips towards Leeming.

'Sign in, please,' he said in a bored voice. 'Here's your key, room four at the top of the stairs and on the left.'

Leeming fished a folded paper out of the inside pocket of his jacket and flattened it onto the desktop with the palm of his hand.

'Have you seen this man?' Sheriff Leeming asked. The clerk half glanced at the grainy picture and shook his head, the sheriff sighed.

'Have a real good look, mister, he's an escaped prisoner and he's killed at least four people.'

While the clerk looked at the poster, the deputy sheriff walked in. Leeming looked across at him but he shook his head. He was twenty-five years younger than Leeming with a face like a baked apple. He moved with suppressed energy, his eyes bright with enthusiasm. He wore a dark blue suit and vest and carried a new Stetson creased down the centre of the crown and he kept running his fingers across the brim. He glanced around the entrance hall, impatient and restless and drummed his fingers on his hat.

The clerk studied the likeness, looked up and said, 'Yes, I saw him yesterday.'

The deputy rushed over but Sheriff Leeming held a hand out, palm up to slow him down. Leeming leaned forward and rested his arms on the counter. 'When did you see him, partner?' he said.

'Yesterday morning, he was here and

he got on the stage.'

'You're sure?' said the deputy.

'Oh yes, I'm certain. The stage left yesterday heading for Chugwater, calling at Powder River. They should reach Powder River tomorrow.'

The sheriff straightened up, looked at his deputy and laughed.

'That boy's a sly dog, ain't he, we weren't looking at the stage. He's riding in style, trying to belly through the brush while we're barking a knot running around the country like a pair of fools.' He turned back to the clerk. 'That's right fine, mister, thanks for the help.' He laid his hand on the clerk's arm and looked at him from under his hat brim. 'You're certain?'

'Positive,' said the clerk, 'the murderer in your wanted poster is one of the passengers on the stage.'

The sheriff and his deputy rode through the night.

5

The blue glow of the early dawn lightened the horizon as the last stars faded in the sky over the staging station. The passengers heard the team brought out and harnessed, the traces jingling in the clear chill morning air.

They had a meal of hot cakes, cold bread, sausages, fried potatoes and plenty of coffee. They ate in silence until the driver called out, 'We've a pull up through the hills before heading down to Powder River. Then it's on to the final stop on this here line at Chugwater.'

'I'm not going with you,' said the buggy driver Jarrett. He sat alone in a corner with his carpet bag on his knees. 'I've just come from the Chugwater area, I'm heading off in the other direction.'

Mason the station manager said, 'You'll have to wait a week for a return stage then.'

'Unless you want to ride your horse

43

bareback and move off on your own?' said Heggarty, wiping his mouth on his sleeve. 'Maybe you can get an Indian to guide for you.'

Jarrett looked around the room and the men surrounding him, he blew out his cheeks in exasperation and rubbed his eyes. Farrington and Heggarty both watched Jarrett with interest; they each had their own reasons for wanting him to stay.

Sorensen mopped his plate with a lump of bread and ignored the conversation around him.

'Give me a ticket for Powder River then, I'll make alternative arrangements from there,' said Jarrett, scowling into the awkward silence. He pressed a dent out of the crown of his hat, straightened the brim and put it on, shading his face so that he could avoid looking at any other passengers.

On the far horizon, the jagged mountain slopes turned lighter against the sky as the sun shot its first warmth of the day across the land and the stage set off. The station master Mason and his stock-tender watched them go, checking that the mule team pulled well. Out of sight behind them a lone rider, Ahiga the Shoshone, also saw all of the passengers on board and watched the dust trail as they left. Then he heeled his horse forward and cantered in an arc, curving around the back of the stage station and, unseen, he followed the stage.

★ ★ ★

By the afternoon the countryside changed as the land became greener, there were more hills and trees, and dark jagged peaks rimmed the horizon. The air cooled a little and a breeze brought the smell of the mountains down across the plains.

The trail forked and the stage slowed and the driver pulled the horses to a stop. A rider blocked the trail. He waited fifty paces away, leading a spare horse with a rifle cradled in his lap and his face hidden by his wide-brimmed, high-crowned

45

straw sombrero pulled down low over his eyes.

The guard lifted his double-barrelled 10-gauge shotgun but the lone rider simply sat and waited. Inside the stage, Farrington sat up and said, 'This is where I get off, friends.' He simply stood, smiled, opened the door and stepped out into the sunlight.

The rider nudged his horse forward down the slope towards the stage as Farrington walked across to meet him. The rider called across.

'There's no problem here, everyone stay where you are, we'll be gone in a minute. My brother's coming with me. It don't mean jack to the rest of you, you all can just get on with your journey.'

Heggarty shrugged to himself and closed his eyes.

Farrington climbed onto the spare horse, a big reddish brown sorrel with a sandy coloured mane and tail; he looked across at his brother.

'A slight change of plan, Fred,' he said. 'There's a fat little feller been delivered to us with a bag of money and maybe a few other trinkets. We'll take that before we high tail it out of here.' Farrington turned to the stage and shouted, 'Everybody out. Nothing stupid, I want the bag that Jarrett's been hugging ever since we picked him up. No heroes and no mule pride stupidity and you can all get on with your day. All step out this side towards me.'

He nodded to his brother and watched as he walked his horse down the other side of the stage.

'My brother has a gun and he'll surely kill anyone stupid enough to try anything. Out now. And you, driver and guard, get on down and join us.' The guard hesitated and Farrington said, 'Stop fooling around or I'll kill you. Look into my eyes and tell me I'm lying.'

Farrington was enjoying himself. He knew that his curly hair and clear skin made him look like a scrub faced Bible seller but it helped in his line of business. That and a smile and a pleasant howdy got him out of many a scrape. If that didn't work he tended to shoot folk.

He came from a God-fearing poor family. He'd always been small, an unimpressive figure who never weighed more than 130 pounds. At fourteen, he ran off and travelled west in a covered wagon with his brother Fred. He stole a gun, a horse and a saddle from a ranch but they caught him and he did eighteen months' jail time. He vowed he would never go back inside. Since then he robbed stagecoaches, rustled cattle and killed at random. He just wanted to be famous like Kit Carson. Pity the man who underestimated him though, he learned to shoot with deadly accuracy and learned to drink with the same enthusiasm. The drink and guns turned him into a quick tempered hell-raiser as bad tempered as a rattlesnake with toothache.

The passengers climbed out and stood in a line in the shadow of the coach with their hands in the air.

'Right,' said Farrington, his deep voice sounding full of rust, 'you, Jarrett, bring that bag over here. Hold it with both hands and walk to me. Don't think about it, just do it. Nobody likes you, mister, so there's no-one going to pull your acorns out of this fire.'

Jarrett shuffled forward, he licked his lips and spoke in a dry cracked voice, as if through a mouthful of pebbles. 'Help me, sir, you're right, I have money,' he pushed the bag forward a little, 'but we can make the people who stole this pay much more. I can take you to them. Let me go with you, I can't go back with the stage; they're looking for me in Powder River.' Farrington glanced at his brother and raised his eyebrows in question.

'Kick him or kill him,' said his brother, 'we need to get gone.'

'Let's not be hasty,' said Farrington, 'maybe he's telling the truth. I knew he was running from something. He panicked and killed an Indian down the trail a piece, we all saw it. He's dirty and up to no good. We'll take him and the money with us and if he's lying, I'll gut him good and we'll still have what he's toting in the bag. You, Jarrett, give me the bag and get your horse unhitched from the back of the stage. Move.'

Jarrett passed the bag up to Farrington and watched him tie it to his saddle horn. Then he went for his own horse, his rumpled shirt hanging out of his trousers and his hands opening and closing at his sides. He rode across like a sack of potatoes and waited.

'Nobody move. I'm Sheriff Lewis Leeming out of Owl Creek, Hot Springs County.'

Farrington and his brother turned in their saddles and saw the sheriff sat on his horse back down the trail, his gun covering the two brothers.

'You heard the man,' said his deputy above and to the side of them as he came into view over a ridge; his voice quivered like a hot wire with bottled up excitement.

'I'm taking you back, Farrington,' said Sheriff Leeming. 'If ever a man deserved to die, it's you. I'll see you hang this time. Now both of you drop your guns or I'll scramble your eggs here and now. You good folks at the stage stay right quiet, this man is wanted for four murders. I'll take him and his no good brother back and you can get about your business.'

The silence and the tension grew. The deputy sheriff ground his teeth and a lump of cartilage flexed in his jaw. Suddenly he snapped, booted his heels into his horse's belly and bolted down the slope.

There was an explosion of noise as the air filled with gunshot, the outlaws opened up on the deputy and sheriff. Deputy Baker, hit in the shoulder and high in the chest, fell over the saddle cantle as if he had jerked backwards on a wire. His horse skidded down the hillside, barrelled into the sheriff and knocked him from his horse, but he rolled and shot from the floor in a hail of lead.

One shot glanced off Farrington's cheekbone in a spray of blood that whipped across his face as his head snapped back. Another caught his brother Fred in the shoulder and he yelled and jerked his horse away up the hill. Farrington sawed on the reins, dragging his own horse after his brother; he ducked low in the saddle as he kicked up the ridge with clods of dirt lifted by the horse's hoofs flying behind him.

The sheriff aimed at his back and pulled the trigger but the hammer snapped drily on an empty chamber. He tried to stand and get his Winchester from the saddle holster but his bad leg gave out under him and he fell back to the ground.

Jarrett rode out, following Farrington and his brother as they disappeared in a cloud of dust and gun smoke. Heggarty watched him leave, he hesitated, torn between stopping Jarrett and making sure the sheriff was unhurt but he knew it was only right to check on the lawman. He ran to help him and his dead deputy. The sheriff hauled himself up off the ground using his horse's stirrup and limped across to where his deputy laid unmoving on the ground. The gun smoke still spun in the sunlight and filled the warm air with the smell of cordite.

Sheriff Leeming wiped his hand across his forehead where a bullet nicked him in the hairline, the wound shallow but leaking blood. He knelt by the dead man and cradled his head in his arms. The deputy's face was as smooth, white and as lifeless as a sheet of paper.

Sheriff Leeming closed his eyes and in a soft voice he said, 'Driver, this man's name is Harland Baker, you take him to the next town and treat him with respect, you hear me?'

'Yes, sir, I guarantee it,' said the driver.

The sheriff reloaded his gun. He put the hammer on half cock, shucked out the empty casings on the floor, rotated the cylinder and inserted six fresh rounds in the loading gate, snapping the gun shut without speaking or looking up.

'I'll come with you, Sheriff, I'd like to help,' said Heggarty. He spoke with quiet determination, his face clustered with anger.

'Why?' said the sheriff, looking him up and down. 'Justice,' said Heggarty.

The sheriff shrugged. 'All right then,'

he said. 'You look like you can use those guns, tell me I'm wrong.'

'I can.'

'I hope so.' He studied Heggarty, he knew there was more to this stranger than met the eye but he had no time to dwell on it and he trusted his own judgement. He liked the look of this slim youngster with his tousled dark hair and his intelligent face bright with colour from the wind. The breeze lifted his jacket and across his waist in a Mexican holster, beautifully engraved in a floral motif, he wore a pair of Smith and Wesson with ancient yellowed ivory grips. He looked as sinewy as a wolf, the sort of man who always checked that the only thing behind him was his shadow.

'Use my deputy's horse. We take Farrington in or we take them down, boy, you understand that?'

'Yes, sir.'

The sheriff called the driver over, he stretched forward in the saddle and leaned his arms across the pommel and the leather creaked under his weight. He pushed his hat up on his brow with his fingers and said, 'Get a message to the nearest town marshal, you tell him Sheriff Leeming sent you. We're out looking for Eugene Farrington and his brother, give him this poster and tell him to get out here and help.'

The sheriff looked over at Heggarty sitting on his deputy's horse, and without speaking he cantered up over the lip of land, kicked off into a gallop and did not look back. Heggarty followed, determined to find out why Jarrett had his mother's brooch and what he knew about his father's death.

6

For the next three hours, the signs were easy to follow and Sheriff Leeming rode them hard, the horses' necks extended and the muscles in their flanks rippling with effort. The plains ran for mile on mile, rolling like an ocean to a horizon lined with hills that stretched upwards into banked clouds bunched on the far slopes.

Eventually Sheriff Leeming slowed his lathered horse to a canter and Heggarty moved alongside him. 'We can't afford to keep this pace up or we'll burn the horses out.'

'Storm coming as well,' said Heggarty, nodding at the clouds.

'Yes, we'll be riding right into it but so are the men we're chasing, we'll lose their trail if it comes in hard. Let's get to the hills for shelter and rest up some.'

'They could be waiting for us.'

'Let's hope so,' said Leeming.

An hour later, they reached the hills and walked their blowing horses down to a slow moving river that skirted the bottom of the first hillside. The incline rose up sheer in front of them, bristling with dark leaved trees.

'Let's break and rest, we need to find shelter. It looks like they crossed over there.' Leeming nodded at the sand-banks across the river, the soil sandy and dark edged with the river's wetness.

'See those tracks?' He pointed at the mud gouged and etched with hoof prints where the riders came out of the water and cut across to a timber lined ridge.

As they looked, the river's surface wrinkled with the breeze and speckled with the first of the rain. The light disappeared and the temperature dropped as the wind rattled the trees and pulled at their hats and coats.

'We'd better sit this one out,' shouted the sheriff, pressing his hat down on his head as they rode for cover.

'We'll lose the trail,' said Heggarty.

'Maybe but we can't push too fast now,

we could ride straight into an ambush. No, we'll take our time, be patient. That's what I always told my deputy but he wouldn't listen and you saw how that ended.'

They sheltered under the cottonwood trees. They had rain slickers in the saddle bags but Sheriff Leeming spread his on the side of a mossy bank and laid dry wood on top of it.

'Cover the lumber with the other slicker, son, we'll have a fire and cook something when the downpour passes.'

The storm blew in, the clouds bunched high and black, the wind swirled and hammered at the canopy above them and thrashed the trees. They had good shelter but the air smelled of moist earth and wet wood.

'This rain's a frog stringer, ain't it?' said the sheriff. He turned and looked at Heggarty. 'What's your story, son, why are you here?'

'I'm heading back home.'

'No, I mean why are you here with me now in this place chasing a wanted killer?'

'Well, my name's Sam Heggarty.' He looked up from under his dripping hat brim. 'I run my own business down at Medicine Bow about a hundred miles south of here. I break horses and sell to the army mostly. My pa owns . . . ' He paused and swallowed. 'My pa did own a small spread between Powder River and Chugwater.'

'He's dead?'

'Yes, my ma wrote to me, he was killed and robbed. I'm here to find who killed him.'

'Sam,' said the sheriff, 'finding Eugene Farrington won't help you. He was under arrest for a week or so before he broke out. That means he wasn't here when your pa was killed.'

Heggarty brushed the water from his trousers and took the brooch out of his pocket.

'It's not Farrington I'm chasing, its Jarrett, the fat little man who rode out with them.'

He explained how they came across

Jarrett by the buggy.

'You see, I found this.' He opened his hand and stretched across, letting the sheriff see the brooch. 'This is my mother's, I'd swear to it. Someone stole it when they killed Pa. I don't know this attorney Jarrett but he had it and I want to know why. There's more stuff in his carpet bag. It sounds like he knows who killed my pa.'

He looked at the brooch beaded with rain in his hand.

'He said he'd take Farrington to the people who killed my pa to get more money out of them.'

Sheriff Leeming nodded.

'I get it, he can lead you to your pa's killers. Farrington will kill him as soon as he gets any more money, maybe sooner if he riles him.'

'Yes, I guessed that, I need to find them before he does.'

'Farrington killed my deputy and four others so I'm going after him full tilt and that means there are no rules. I'm taking Farrington down, son, you understand

60

that?' said Leeming.

'I do, sure. I hope to keep Jarrett alive, though, at least for a while.'

The clouds swept away, the rain ticked the leaves, the temperature rose and the sun pushed back out.

'Let's eat,' said Leeming. 'I've food in my bags.'

They walked their horses out of the broken light under the steaming trees into the sunshine and made a rough camp.

While Sheriff Leeming stowed the slickers in the saddle bags, Heggarty lit a fire with the dry wood. Leeming limped back, he smelled coffee boiling and pork frying. Heggarty squatted on his haunches by the fire pit, stirring strips of bacon in a skillet, his eyes squinting against the light smoke. He held out a plate for the sheriff filled with bacon and hunks of bread fried in the bacon fat. Leeming cut into the meat and soaked up the hot grease with the bread.

They ate in silence then Leeming wiped his fingers on the back of his trousers, stretched out on a cushion of tangled grass and sat with a lump of chewing tobacco wadded in his cheek. He massaged his leg, looked up and saw Heggarty watching him.

'The war,' he said, his teeth coloured like charcoal from the plug of tobacco, 'the Battle of Bull Run. A Sunday as I recall, the drums beat assembly and in ten minutes, we marched off. We advanced double quick time and our company went into thick woods. As soon as we got in there a volley scythed through us. A few of us rallied together but they hit us with a storm of bullets then round shot and shell poured on us and tore us to pieces. I was one of the lucky ones.'

Heggarty studied the sun on the water's rippled surface while the sheriff chewed on his tobacco wad then Leeming grunted as he stood and said, 'Let's clean up and make something happen.'

As they rode away the sheriff looked back over his shoulder.

'There's somebody else out here, boy,

I can feel it in my bones.'

The sun went behind a cloud, blanketing the land in shadow.

7

Across country, Marshal Marcello stood next to the abandoned buggy. They had been searching for Jarrett ever since he ran from the Heggarty killing.

'It's his all right, I don't know where he was holed up these last couple of days but he's moving now.' He looked down the trail towards Moneta. The trail was corrugated with wheel tracks.

'Jarrett must have taken the horse and headed back the way he'd come. We must've missed him when we cut across country. I can't see any sign that he rode on to Moneta and he's too green to risk open country.'

Marshal Marcello glanced at Stanton. He stared at his cruel face, his nose mashed almost flat and to the left, giving him a lopsided appearance like a clenched fist. He looked like a man whose life had been one long bad day. Marcello knew he was as big as life and twice as mean.

He scared Marcello. Stanton and the Colonel both looked at him and seemed to know he lived a lie. Marcello did not have the guts to be a town marshal and he knew it, he suspected they did too. He'd walked into the job by accident.

He was a temporary deputy and went with the real marshal to serve a warrant on two local farmers. The men were wanted in connection with a murder. They found the two of them in a small settlement ten miles outside of Powder River. A gunfight erupted and as the shooting started, Marcello fled and hid in a barn. The marshal was wounded in the chest but carried on and shot one of the men. The second one rushed up and hit him with an axe. The marshal gunned him down but they both died. Marcello came out when it quietened down. When the dust settled, everyone thought he had killed the gunmen, well, maybe he exaggerated his part in it. Next thing he knew, he was town marshal with a reputation as a man mean enough to hunt bears with a hickory stick. Powder River was a quiet place so it worked until Stanton appeared. Now he had a whole mess of grief. The worry made him ill, his stomach either felt like it was burning up inside or as if someone twisted a knife into his guts.

'The stage passed by, maybe Jarrett got on that,' said Stanton.

'Could be,' said Marcello he studied the traces in the trail dust. 'The stage stopped and they all walked around some. There's a swing station down there, let's find out if they saw him.' He stopped as he walked back to his horse.

'Wait.' He pointed to the ground. 'There's blood by the wheel and some by the trail over yonder.' He pointed with his chin. The blood lay caked with dust and swarming with flies.

'Maybe he's dead?' said Stanton.

Marshal Marcello studied the floor and shrugged. 'It'd be good if he was because it would save you the trouble of killing him. But we want what he stole in that goddamn bag and it's not here.

Let's get to that stage station.'

If you hadn't been so goddamn trigger happy and enjoyed killing so much, you wouldn't have frightened him off when you shot old Heggarty, thought Marcello but he kept his thoughts to himself. He knew that you didn't rile Ned Stanton, not unless you were tired of living or very fast with a gun and Marcello knew he wasn't either of those things.

8

After the storm, Heggarty and Sheriff Leeming continued their search for Farrington and Jarrett. They followed a winding dirt track through a golden meadow to a canyon with another river roaring across its boulder-strewn base. The trail followed the river and they rode upwards, following the gradient under cliffs and trees that grew in awkward clumps out of the tumbled rocks until the river was far below.

The rains wiped the trail of any signs of the riders, the wash off the hills littered the track with dead leaves, small stones and puddles that glittered in the sunlight. Sheriff Leeming's horse slithered sideways on the shale just as a shot rang out, the crack echoing over their heads and lifting birds out of the trees. The sheriff toppled from his saddle and fell in an untidy heap.

'Get back against the trees,' he shouted.

He dragged himself into the lee of a rock, his left hand tangled in his reins and he pulled his horse towards him.

'Are you hurt?' said Heggarty.

'Of course I'm goddamn hurt, boy. Look, the shot came from those rocks to the right of the track down yonder.'

'I'll try and get the drop on him,' said Heggarty and he grabbed his Spencer rifle from the saddle holster, checked he had a seven-round tube magazine in the stock and ducked into the trees.

As he moved away he heard the sheriff say, 'Be careful, they may have just tried to slow us and moved on but they could be waiting for you.' Heggarty stayed silent and ran holding his rifle two-handed across his chest, the wet undergrowth brushed against his trousers and glistened across his boots.

He looked down through the trees to where the rocks below were bathed in a brittle yellow sunlight but he could not see much with the sun glare in his eyes. He reached open ground at the bottom and sprinted through the bright sunshine to the base of the rocks without seeing any movement.

He paused to catch his breath and heard a boot scrape the rocks above his head and dirt showered down onto his hat and back.

'You should have stayed with the stage, partner,' said a voice from above.

He looked up and Farrington's brother stood over him, silhouetted against the sun.

Heggarty rolled but before he could fire, an arrow whooshed from the trees and skewered the man on the rocks. The arrow head buried deep in his throat. His gun fell from his hand as he scrambled for the arrow shaft, his eyes wide with disbelief. He pitched forward and crashed down from above like a lump of rock, hitting the dirt with a dull thud.

Ahiga the Shoshone stepped from the trees, a hickory bow in his hands.

Ahiga smiled at Heggarty and walked towards him. His arrows were in a hide quiver across his back. His hair braided with beads now, he wore a sleeveless faded blue shirt with its tail hanging out of his trousers. He slid like the shadow of a cat across the grass without making a sound, his moccasins strapped over his trousers and up over his knees; he moved with barely a limp from his earlier wound.

'Thank you, Ahiga,' said Heggarty.

Ahiga pulled the arrow out, stuck the arrow head in the ground to clean it and slipped it into his quiver.

'Other men gone,' said Ahiga, 'we follow.' Heggarty relaxed. 'Yes, soon, I must help my friend, he's hurt back there.'

'Brother's bow,' said Ahiga, holding the bow out. 'You honour him, Ahiga. Come with me,' said Heggarty, pointing back up the trail. 'My friend is a sheriff, he can help you.'

'No, I will follow the other men, find man who killed my brother.' He held his hand over his heart. 'Revenge.' His copper skin stretched tight across his high cheekbones and his arm muscles flexed and tightened like iron.

'Listen,' said Heggarty, 'I think the

man you are chasing knows who killed my father. I must talk to him, it's important that I get his bag.' He used his hands to shape a bag to help Ahiga understand. 'I must find out who killed my pa.' Ahiga pointed at Heggarty smiled and said, 'Revenge?'

'Yes, revenge for me as well,' Heggarty said with a nod. 'But I need the man alive first and his bag, understand?'

Ahiga shrugged his shoulders. He turned away and as the shadows of the trees swallowed him up, without looking back, he said, 'Life of a Shoshone is like the wings of the air. The hawk knows how to get his prey. Shoshone is like that. Hawk swoops down on prey and so does Ahiga. In your tongue, Ahiga means he fights.'

Heggarty rode back up the trail on the dead man's horse with the body draped across the saddle and found Sheriff Leeming where he had left him, lying down smoking a pipe.

'How's the leg?'

'Wooden,' said the sheriff, he tapped

his shin with his pipe. 'Lost it nearly up to the knee at Bull Run, a shell took it clean off. That shot just then caught it near the top, punched into the wood and splintered it into my knee. Hurts like hell but it stopped the bullet hitting me in the guts. I need to pad the stump properly before I get after them. What happened?' He stood, hobbled over and lifted the dead man's head by the hair. 'It's the brother, Fred as I recall.' He hesitated, looking at the throat wound. 'Looks like an arrow killed him.' Heggarty told him what had happened. Sheriff Leeming scratched his cheek with his finger and said, 'I knew someone was bird-dogging us. I used to get the same feeling in the war when Johnny Reb followed us. Didn't nobody else reckon it but me. Ahiga took him down hard then.'

'Yes. Ahiga is a good man but I guess we both know that we keep him out of this. I reckon there's plenty around here don't want to hear that a Shoshone killed a white man, whatever the reason. For some folk there's no reason good enough for that.' Sheriff Leeming nodded and Heggarty continued. 'I've got to get after them, I need to talk to Jarrett. I can't let Ahiga kill him. Not yet anyway.'

'OK, son, I get it, you go on. I'll follow when I can.' Heggarty pointed off east and said, 'If you ride down that way you'll hit the main trail, follow it on to Powder River. We're all heading for Powder River one way or another.

Sheriff Leeming struggled to climb on his horse. The strain obvious, his face was the colour of grey ash. Heggarty looked at him with concern and sighed.

'I'd best come with you. We'll head straight for Powder River. I'll see you get back in one piece. The rest will have to wait.'

Sheriff Leeming's voice sounded thick and tired when he said, 'I'm sorry, boy, I'm too weak to argue. I know you need to get after them. Farrington will kill Jarrett as soon as he can, he's as mean as a lonely rooster. And now the Shoshone's tracking them both and aims to kill Jarrett.'

'Seems like no-one wants Jarrett alive except me.'

9

Eugene Farrington rode on with Jarrett while his brother Fred stopped to ambush Sheriff Leeming.

Behind them they heard Fred's shot. Farrington smiled, his eyes as cold as buckshot. They slowed their horses.

'That's Fred, that goddamn sheriff must've followed us.'

They listened for a second shot or return fire but time ticked by without any more gunfire. Farrington hit his saddle horn with a fist and laughed.

'Goddamn it, Fred's got him for sure. I hope it was right between the eyes. Come on, Jarrett, ride, things just got a whole lot better for the both of us. Let's put some gone between us and that dead sheriff. Fred will find us later. Come on, you should be grinning like a weasel in a hen house, get that sour look off your face — you're still alive, ain't you? Don't you annoy me, you with me on that?'

Jarrett looked at Farrington's back with hatred and cursed his luck. He hadn't wanted any part in the murder of Walter Heggarty and he managed to escape from the trouble in Powder River. He thought he'd made it clear away, it was just bad luck when the buggy wheel came off. Then he'd panicked when the Indian picked up his bag and he shot one of them. He knew he'd made a mistake when the stage pulled up. He'd got out of that tight spot but his troubles just kept on coming.

He whipped his reins across the horse's shoulders and raced after Farrington, too scared to do anything else but follow.

They clattered down into a huge valley where the river reappeared, swirling down the valley floor with deep banks littered with boulder and rock webbed with lichen.

They went along the riverside, following as it curved and undercut the rocks towering above it on the far side.

'Into the water,' shouted Farrington and they slid down the high banking and plunged into the icy water. The horses barrelled against the current with the water chest high as they surged into the middle of the river. Farrington grabbed the reins off Jarrett and dragged him in his wake, urging them on towards the far cliff face.

The overhang loomed above them and they pushed under the crag into the dark cold shadows. The horses floundered but found solid footing on a rock shelf that ran beneath the water's dark surface and they pulled themselves out of the water into a hidden cave. They stood dripping and gasping, spokes of sunlight shone down into the cave through the gaps in the rocks overhead. The walls ran with water that shone like ice in the light from above.

'Fred was right, no-one will find us here, we're safe. Well, I'm safe, we'll have to see about you,' said Farrington. 'Pull yourself together, you look like a raccoon that drowned in a rain barrel. There's food and kindling back yonder, we'll dry off and wait for my brother.'

He drew his gun. 'Don't try anything, I can use you but I'll kill you if I have to and enjoy doing it.' Farrington's mouth twisted into a smile as he spoke and then he laughed and shivered like a mad dog.

They took their jackets off and dried themselves by a fire, the flames whipping in the down draught.

'I'm going to tie you so that we can both get some sleep while we wait. I don't know what's happened to Fred, maybe he's having trouble but he knows where we are.'

A couple of hours later, Jarrett woke Farrington up. 'I need the toilet,' pleaded Jarrett. He lay hog-tied hand and foot but Farrington ignored him and opened the bag and rummaged around inside it. 'What the hell's all this paper?' he said, looking at Jarrett.

'Contracts, read them and you'll see.'

'I don't read,' said Farrington. 'I can hide behind a newspaper but it don't mean I read.' He glared at Jarrett, becoming hostile and tense by the moment. 'I done told you once, don't rile me, mister, just tell me what it's all about or when I'm done with you there won't be enough left of you to snore.'

'They're land contracts. They show who owns pieces of land around Powder River and Chugwater. These contracts are new ones.'

'Why? What's been going on?' Jarrett decided to tell the truth.

'The town marshal in Powder River is called Marcello, him and a hired gun called Stanton have been driving folk off the land for someone called Colonel DeVere. Then all of the land will be sold for big money. They murdered a farmer. Now they want to kill me because I saw them do it. And I have this bag with papers they want and what they stole from the dead man.'

'I get it - you're the witness that might squeal like a stuck pig.'

'Well, I wouldn't quite put it like that.'

'I would and I know what I'd do to you if I was them. So what have you got in mind?' said Farrington. 'Remember you're only here and alive because you can buy your way out.'

Jarrett said, 'You go to Stanton with a letter from me. It'll say I'll keep quiet if they pay me off. When they agree we arrange a swap. So then a few days later, you give them the bag when they give you the money. You'll be able to handle him, won't you?'

Farrington ignored the question. 'And then?'

'You let me go,' said Jarrett. 'Maybe I can keep a bit of the money?'

'Maybe,' said Farrington, his rasping voice a hollow echo off the cave walls. 'I ain't against it. In fact, I like it real good. A town marshal and a gunslinger eating out of my hand. I could make things as hot as a whore-house on nickel night for them. Write the letter, and draw a map so I can get where I'm going.'

He untied Jarrett's hands and when he'd finished writing, Jarrett said, 'This tells them what to do. Tell them I sent you, I'm Buford Jarrett, an attorney and I saw them kill Walt Heggarty.'

Farrington slid the letter into the inside pocket of his jacket. 'You're staying here and you're staying tied up until I come back or Fred turns up. When he does, you tell him where I am.' He drew his gun and whipped the butt across Jarrett's head, retied his hands and headed out through the watery entrance.

★ ★ ★

The Shoshone Ahiga trailed Farrington and Jarrett, he read their sign and came after them. He followed their tracks to the river and saw them outlined in the mud on the bank where they entered the water.

He could not find any traces on the far bank and thought they must have ridden up or downstream in the water to hide their tracks. He rode downstream for a few hours, scanning the bank until the river deepened and rushed over a waterfall. He knew now that they did not go downstream and so he turned and made his way back to where they had crossed.

On the way back upstream he heard the jingle of a bridle, the creak of saddle leather and the thud of shoed horses on the path and he pulled away and hid in a copse of trees. He dragged his pony down to the ground in dappled shadows where a thick layer of black leaves matted the ground and lay with him, his hand resting on the pony's nose. The riders were a couple of strangers on big boned swaybacked mules that looked like they had seen a lot of miles. Ahiga rested and set off back in the late afternoon and missed Farrington set off from the cave to deliver the letter.

When Ahiga got back to the river crossing by the hidden cave, he saw the fresh tracks that Farrington made in the last hour and puzzled over them. He dismounted on top of the hill and prayed to the Great Spirit for guidance; he sang in the language of his ancestors.

'The Great Spirit is in all things. He is in the air we breathe. The Great Spirit is our Father, but the Earth is our Mother. She nourishes us. What is life? It is the flash of a firefly in the night. It is the breath of a buffalo in the wintertime. It is the little shadow which runs across the grass and loses itself in the sunset.'

He thought, two horses went into the water many hours ago and one horse came out late in the afternoon. That means that one horse and rider are still in the river. How could that happen? And where had the other rider been?

And then his head came up and he smelt wood smoke like a faint breath in the grass where he sat. The smoke came from the earth at his feet, trickling up through the rocks and undergrowth from below.

He smiled and thanked his spirit guide. He knew the answer was a hidden cave beneath him. The entrance must be in the water.

He waded into the river with his knife in his hand. In the middle, the water reached his chest, the coldness climbed into his shoulders and neck. The current dragged at his legs and pushed him into the shadows under the rocks.

He lost his footing and went under with the cold water sucking and pushing at him but he felt no fear. He kicked out and pushed into the blackness that surrounded him. His hands found the rock shelf and he pulled himself forward. His head bobbed above the surface and he glimpsed a horse and his brother's killer tied up against the cave wall.

He surged to his feet with the water streaming out of his hair, his wet clothes moulded to his lean muscular body.

Jarrett screamed when he saw a figure rear up out of the river, water cascading off his head and body. He watched in wide-eyed fascination as the wet shadow stepped forward and the Indian he had shot stood before him with a knife in his hand.

Ahiga knelt next to Jarrett, grabbed his hair and pulled his head back. He placed the knife point next to Jarrett's eye. He pushed on the blade and the point sank into the crumpled flesh and a drop of blood welled up by the knife tip and rolled down Jarrett's cheek like a bright red tear.

'I take your eyes then in death you will not find the ghost trail. You wander forever in the spirit world. My brother's revenge.'

As the night closed in outside, Jarrett found his voice and screamed but there was only Ahiga to hear him beg for his life.

10

Across country, Farrington found Stanton's cabin. It was a single-storey clapboard frame house. He sat on his horse in a stand of black oak trees and looked down at it. The cabin looked badly weathered and neglected. The barn roof sagged and a wooden bridge across a creek at the back greyed with age, the planking hung down with slatted gaps that had not been replaced. A couple of saddled horses stood tethered to the rail out front of the cabin, their tails flicking at the flies in the early evening sun.

Farrington nudged his horse down, pulled his rifle out and held it across his lap. He could feel them watching him from inside and as he stopped his horse twenty paces from the door, it swung open and a man stepped onto the veranda.

'What do you want?' Stanton said in a voice as hard as a punch.

'I'm looking for Stanton.'

'You've found him, now state your business.'

'I've got a message for you,' said Farrington and he took Jarrett's note from his jacket pocket and waved it in the air with his left hand.

'A message from who exactly?'

'Buford Jarrett,' said Farrington; he saw Stanton tense and clump down the steps. He walked across to Farrington and snatched the paper out of his hand.

'Marcello,' he called over his shoulder and the town marshal stepped out of the shadows under the porch and took the note. Farrington noticed the star pinned to his jacket but he did not react other than to nod at the newcomer.

Marcello wore a black woollen jacket and a grey vest. He was average height but built like a barrel. His eyes locked on Farrington's face and stayed there before he looked down at the note. As he read the message, a muscle worked in his jawline and he bit the skin on his finger and spat it out. Farrington's horse grew restless, snorted, pitched its head against the bridle and stepped sideways a couple of paces.

'Do I know you?' said Marshal Marcello, looking him up and down.

'Look, I'm just delivering a message. I know what the note says. If you want the bag back and for us to keep quiet about the man you killed, then you pay us off.'

'You'll be Farrington,' said Stanton. 'Don't look so surprised, we talked to the stagecoach driver earlier today in Powder River. We know who you are and what you've done.'

Farrington looked pleased that they knew who he was.

'That's right, friends, I'm the Eugene Farrington you all heard about. I don't give a hill of beans who you two are. You'd better pay. I'll be back in three days' time to collect. It says all of that in the note.'

To his surprise, Marcello grinned and said, 'Yes, Jarrett's told us what to do.'

'Then just stick to the deal.'

'Oh we'll do that, we surely will,' said

Marcello, 'you'll get yours in three days, now get gone.'

Farrington flushed bright red with anger, pointed at Marcello and said in a voice that rumbled like someone dragging a spade across stone, 'Don't you talk to me like that, fat boy, I might rope you and put you with the other hogs.'

Marcello stumbled back in shock, sweat stood out on his forehead like a freshly watered pumpkin. Farrington turned to look at Stanton but the big man had a face that looked to be chiselled out of granite. Stanton yawned, turned his back on Farrington, pushed Marcello into the cabin and slammed the door behind him.

The two men watched Farrington ride away. Marcello said, 'The note says he'll be back. Jarrett says that boy can't read so he has no idea what's really happening. According to Jarrett they'll come back in three days. We pay $5,000 and Jarrett gives us the bag and promises to get out of the territory. He'll bring Farrington along and wants us to kill him.' He put a hand to his stomach and winced. 'I feel like I'm sitting on a goddamn powder keg. What are we going to do?'

'Think,' said Stanton. 'There'll be more than one killing around here if everything works out right, but it may take a bit more time yet before I can lead these folk to hell. I'll tell you one thing for sure, I ain't met a problem yet I cain't solve with a gun.'

★　★　★

Farrington felt ten feet tall as he rode away, he laughed to himself at the sight of the town marshal backing off in fear. He checked the map and saw that with a slight detour he could reach Powder Creek just around dark. He smiled to himself, he had money from the bag and he decided to head into town for some fun.

An hour later, he left his horse at the rail on the outskirts and strolled down the sidewalk towards the noise of the nearest saloon. Sam Heggarty missed him by five minutes when he crossed to the bath house. Heggarty arrived with the injured Sheriff Leeming about an hour earlier and decided to clean himself up while the doctor tended to Leeming.

He paid his dollar for the hot bath and towel. The Chinese attendant disappeared out back where a big metal drum over a fire pit heated the water drawn from the pump. Heggarty slipped into a cubicle and undressed. The attendant came in with a bucket of scalding water and poured it in. Heggarty closed his eyes, cleaned out an ear with his little finger and dozed in the heat and the steam.

He heard another customer come in and go down the room to the last cubicle, he could hear the murmur of voices and then the sound of water being sluiced over someone and a rasping voice he immediately recognized said, 'Nice and hot, partner and bring me a whiskey, right quick.'

It was Farrington. Heggarty was fully awake now, he eased himself out of the water and dressed as quietly as he could. He drew back the heavy curtain and padded out carrying his boots. His shirt and trousers were pasted to his wet body, his hat pushed down over his damp hair, water ran down the back of his neck and under his crumpled collar.

He backed down the passageway, fumbled his boots on, nodded to the Chinese attendant and slipped out into the night.

He shivered when the cooling night air coiled around him but he ignored it and ran across the street, ducking into the shadowed alleyway opposite the bath house. It seemed that the darkness enveloped and protected him, the dusty floor looked like velvet in the corridor of the alley. He waited.

Fifteen minutes later, the bath house door opened and Farrington stood etched against the lamplight. He ran his fingers through his hair and pushed his hat on, slanted down on his forehead. As Heggarty started forward, a wagon and team of four lurched around the corner and trundled down the street, blocking his view of the bath house door. When it passed by, the doorway stood empty, Farrington had gone.

Heggarty ran into the street and saw Farrington entering the saloon further down. He eased the hammer back on his Smith and Wesson and rushed over to the saloon window. It had the usual wooden boardwalk in front, powdered with dust a step higher than the street and a long hitching post out front.

He pressed his face up to the glass, cupped his hands around his eyes and saw the small figure of Farrington standing at the bar. The saloon was bright, crowded and noisy, the sounds resonating down the glass. The usual crowd of drovers, failed prospectors, saddle tramps and drummers allowed themselves to be fleeced until they were stony-broke and then, as soon as they had money again, back they came for more.

Heggarty turned as he heard boots loud on the plank sidewalk behind him and to his surprise he saw Sorensen, from the stagecoach, about to enter the saloon.

'Sorensen,' he said.

Sorensen looked up and as recognition lit his eyes, his face clouded with doubt and he took a step backwards, let out his breath but did not speak.

'I need your help,' said Heggarty, 'you remember the murderer Farrington from the stage? Well, he's at the bar. I need you to get the town marshal and bring him over here, I'll keep an eye on Farrington.'

'I won't do nothing for you,' said Sorensen, the leathery skin of his face cobwebbed with wrinkles.

Heggarty fumbled in his pockets and pulled out some money.

'Here's about ten dollars, take it and get the marshal over here. Now.'

Sorensen grabbed the money and crumpled it in his hand.

'Look,' said Heggarty and he pointed into the saloon, 'Farrington's picked up a woman and he's heading up the stairs. Get the goddamn marshal.' Without waiting for an answer, Heggarty pushed his way into the saloon, rushed across the room and disappeared up the stairs.

Sorensen waited until Heggarty moved out of sight and strolled to the bar.

'Beer again?' said the bartender.

'No,' said Sorensen, 'not this time. Line me up one of those bourbons and make sure it isn't any of that watered down red eye liquor you fill with turps and gunpowder.'

Heggarty turned the corner in the stairs. He slid a Smith and Wesson out, lifted it free of his coat and held it down at his side as he reached the landing. The hallway was a long one with a series of doors on both sides and a single lamp at the far end.

The only room with a closed door was at the front by the window. He glanced into the other rooms as he worked his way down the building but there was no-one in sight, just beds with dirty bedclothes thrown across them. A man in a strap undershirt with his suspenders hanging over his hips stepped out of a doorway and stared at Heggarty with the gun in his hand. The man backed into the room and softly closed the door. Heggarty ignored him and when he reached the end of the landing, he glanced out of the window, hoping to see the marshal moving in, but the street looked deserted. He could not hear anyone coming up the stairs, he cursed Sorensen and decided not to wait.

He stood outside the room and looked at the bottom of the door and through the gap, he saw a shadow move across the light. Heggarty did not hesitate, he threw his weight against the door as he turned the handle and rushed into the room like a burst of hot sunshine.

Farrington sat on the side of the bed, stripped to the waist and pulling his boots off. The muscles in his arms were so thick and corded they looked like they were full of concrete. His gun belt lay on a scarred wooden table next to the door. Farrington spoke with a relaxed grin.

'Well, look, it's my buddy from the stage and I've left my rig by the door, I must have my mind on other things.'

He pointed with his head to the other side of the room where a hard faced red-haired woman stood with her hands on her hips. She wore a bright mauve ruffled short skirt and her shoulders were bare above a low-cut bodice.

'I don't know what the hell's going on here but this boy's got a whole lot on his mind. And I ain't been paid yet, I'm . . .'

Heggarty turned, looked at her and raised his finger to his lips to quieten her. Farrington took his chance, jumped off the bed and grabbed Heggarty, his powerful hand knotted Heggarty's shirt in his fist and he head butted him. Farrington was the smaller of the two men and his forehead caught Heggarty on the chin, snapping his head back. Then Farrington wrapped a leg around the back of Heggarty's knee and pushed him, knocking the gun from his hand as they both fell over.

Farrington clamped his hands on Heggarty's throat, they felt hard and rough like pieces of sawn lumber and Heggarty could feel his pulse throbbing behind his eyes from the pressure. He shifted his weight and threw the smaller man sideways and slammed Farrington's head against the bed frame with a jolt that shook his teeth. Heggarty stood and dragged Farrington up with him.

Heggarty smacked him on the head with a swinging roundhouse punch and followed through with a right hook that was meant for the chin but caught Farrington in the throat and laid him out. Heggarty took no chances, he stooped over the unconscious body and drove his fist as hard as he could into his thick neck.

When Farrington came round he sat up on the edge of the bed, a red bubble of saliva stained his chin and he held the back of his wrist against his mouth. He hung his head between his legs and spat. He looked at his saliva, stained red with his blood, hanging in strings from his lips. He wiped a smear of blood off his nose with the back of his hand and said, 'You're heck on wheels right enough. I feel like I've got a furnace in my head.'

He looked up, the woman had gone and Heggarty leaned against the wall with his gun levelled at Farrington.

'The marshal's on his way,' said Heggarty, 'he should have been here by now but I guess my first message didn't get delivered. Anyway, I sent the woman, I paid her out of the money in your jacket. Get dressed.'

He threw him his shirt and jacket.

Heggarty stared at him with a look as still and certain as a cocked rifle and said, 'After that fight at the stage this morning you lit out with a fat man in tow called Jarrett, where is he?'

Farrington pulled at his ear and made a pretence of thinking.

'Jarrett, fat man ... no, I don't rightly recall any of that. You must be mixing me up with some other good looking feller.'

The talk stalled when they heard someone coming down the corridor, the door opened and a deputy, not the marshal, came in.

'What's going on?' said the deputy, looking at Heggarty.

He was a young man, rail thin with jug ears and a tall, round-topped pale blue Stetson. It was a lot of hat, in fact, he looked more hat than man, thought Heggarty as he said, 'This is Eugene Farrington, wanted on four counts of murder.'

'Five now, don't forget the deputy.' Farrington smirked.

'Sheriff Leeming out of Owl Creek wants him holding until he's finished with the doctor. He'll be along in the morning.'

They took Farrington down to the jail house and locked him up. The deputy promised to tell Sheriff Leeming and make a full report to the town marshal when he got back.

'We'll talk in the morning, Farrington,' said Heggarty as he left.

'I wouldn't count on it,' muttered Farrington. He lay back on the bed with his hands behind his head. With what he knew about the marshal, he felt sure they had to let him go. It turned out he was half right.

11

Later that night, Marshal Marcello poked his head around the jail house door and saw his deputy drinking coffee and leafing through a pile of Wanted posters at the desk.

'Learned to read, Jake?' said Marcello.

The deputy looked up, leaned back in his chair and hooked his thumbs in his gun belt, he looked mighty pleased with himself.

'Marshal, how do. I'm looking through these, trying to find a match for the prisoner.' He jerked his head backwards towards the cell and let cigarette smoke drift through his teeth. 'And I'm right pleased because I've just found him.' He pushed the poster across the desk and tapped the picture.

Marcello read the poster and forced a smile, he read out, '*Eugene Farrington, age twenty-two, height five feet two inches, light curly hair, blue eyes and even features. The above reward will be paid for his capture or positive proof of his death. Wanted for the crime of murder.'*

Stanton looked over Marcello's shoulder but he kept quiet.

'I brought him in, Marshal,' said the deputy, looking up. He scrapped a finger nail between his teeth and sucked on what he found.

Marcello and Stanton ignored him and walked to the cell door and looked through the bars.

They saw Farrington sat on the bunk with a coffee in his hand and a cigarette in his mouth. He looked up at them through the layers of drifting cigarette smoke and said, 'Do I know you?' Repeating what Marcello had said to him earlier in the day, he spoke without taking the cigarette from his mouth and smiled through the smoke.

'Let's take this outside, Jake,' said Marcello to his deputy. He turned back to Farrington and pointed at him. 'You keep quiet, understand?'

Farrington nodded and lay out on the bunk with his arm across his eyes.

After the deputy told them the full story, Marcello sent him off to give Sheriff Leeming the news. Marcello rolled himself a cigarette, picked a piece of tobacco off his tongue then lit up. He leaned his back against a post and said in a harsh whisper, 'This is all going to hell. Jarrett's still out there. Now we have Farrington locked in the jail and a County Sheriff in town. What are we going to do?' He began to chew on his fingernail.

Stanton bit a lump out of a plug of tobacco and said, 'The first problem is the County Sheriff, we don't want him poking his nose in. If we give him Farrington, he'll go.' He hawked a gob of tobacco juice into the dust and added, 'But we don't want Farrington to spill the beans to this Sheriff Leeming about the murder.' Stanton put both hands on to the hitching rail, leaned forward and winked. 'I can guarantee Farrington won't talk. We'll deliver him to the sheriff right enough. But he won't talk because he'll be dead when we hand him over. There's no reason for the sheriff to stay then. You go and tell Farrington you'll help him bust out. We'll be waiting for him with a fist full of lead.'

Marcello nodded and went back inside the jail house. He rummaged around in a desk drawer and found an old Cooper Pocket revolver, the metal shiny and smooth with holster wear. He opened the loading gate and thumbed five rounds in. He spun the cylinder with the palm of his hand so that Farrington could see and hear what he did.

'We're getting you out, Farrington, because you've got too much on us, I'm giving you this gun. When the deputy comes back, we'll leave you to it. You'll be able to handle the kid, wait an hour or so then kill him or stick him in the cell and get gone. Where's your horse?'

'Never you mind where my horse is at,' said Farrington, his flat savage eyes locked on Marcello as he spoke. 'You get out of here when the deputy comes back. I'll do this my own way. You just have that money ready in three days.'

When the deputy returned, he told them that Sheriff Leeming was as happy as a hog in slop. Marcello and Stanton left, crossed the street and stood in front of the saloon.

'I'll walk down to the end by the livery,' murmured Stanton, 'you cover the other way.'

Inside, Farrington did not wait, he made his move. 'Hey, kid,' he shouted, 'how about another coffee, huh?' He rattled his cup on the metal bars and held it out through the bars. As the deputy reached for it, Farrington snatched his wrist with his free hand and pulled him forward, grabbed his collar and hauled his head hard against the metal bars. His strong hard hands and thick wrists ridged with bone had a grip like a vice. The blood drained from the deputy's face as Farrington clamped him tight against the cell door.

Farrington used one hand to pull the gun from the waistband at the back of his trousers. His knuckles whitened as he pressed his hand tighter on the gun butt. He thumbed the hammer back and pushed the barrel into the deputy's cheek.

'Listen, I'm going to swing anyway so killing you don't mean jack to me. I'm going to let go of you and I want you to fetch the key and unlock this door. If you try to run out on me. I'll plug you good. Do you understand?'

The deputy's eyes were hot and bright, moisture beaded his top lip, he tried to speak but he swallowed and his voice caught in his throat.

'First,' said Farrington, 'pull your gun out and toss it through the bars in here. Look at me, look in my eyes and tell me I'm bluffing. Do it now.'

The gun clattered to the floor by Farrington's feet and he kicked it away against the wall. As Farrington let him go, the deputy backed away a pace, a red circle where the barrel had pressed into the pale skin of his cheek, his big hat pushed down crookedly on the side of his head.

'I can see the keys on the desk,' said Farrington in a quiet voice. 'Get them and open the cell door. If you go past that desk or make a noise I'll drill you right good.'

The deputy blinked, his eyes burning like he had grit under the lids, a drop of sweat rolled out of his hair into his eye and he wiped it with the palm of his hand. He brought the key, unlocked the door and Farrington pulled it open.

'Step in here,' said Farrington. He held his revolver two-handed as steady as a rock, aimed at the deputy's heaving chest.

'Sit on the bed, son, I don't want any noise so I won't shoot unless you do something real stupid.'

The deputy slumped down on the bed, there was a sound in his ears like wind blowing in a low cave. Farrington stepped over and swiped the gun sideways across the deputy's temple and he rolled across the bunk. Farrington locked an arm around the unconscious deputy's neck, with his other hand he grabbed his head and wrenched his neck sideways, it broke with a dry snap. Farrington undid the deputy's gun rig and tied it around his own waist, picked up his gun and walked back to the jail doorway. He looked back, his eyes filled with death; he put his hat on and said, 'Hell comes wherever I hang my hat, boy, folks would do well to remember that.'

He eased the door open and listened. He drew a deep breath, enjoying the tension and he smiled to himself and surged through the door. He ran, hugging the shadows that crowded the front of the building, his boots thumping across the buckled and broken spaces in the planking.

No sooner was he out of the door than gunshots rang out from the shadows across the street. He saw the muzzle flashes, they lit up the squat solid bulk of Marcello. The bullets thunked into the wooden sidewalk and buildings as he passed. Farrington tripped on the uneven surface and it saved his life as the bullets ripped above him, peppering the wall. He rolled and scrambled to his feet; the silence told him Marcello needed to reload and he made it to his horse, whipped the reins loose and leapt on as it moved away. He lay low in the saddle with the saddle horn digging into his chest as the horse responded and surged away out of town.

Marcello moved into the middle of the street and emptied his gun into the mushrooming cloud of sound and dust as Farrington made his escape. Stanton hurried up just as the saloon doors flew open and eight or nine drinkers crowded out onto the sidewalk. They stood milling around, shouting and waving their revolvers. Marcello hurried across to his office, came back out and called, 'The prisoner's out and he's killed young Jake.'

Most of the inebriated crowd outside the saloon knew the deputy and they howled in anger.

'Get after him,' someone shouted, 'let's string him up.'

It only took a moment or two and half a dozen of them grabbed horses and

110

thundered down the trail in a haze of bloodlust, revenge and alcohol.

Stanton stared with dark baleful eyes, his face covered with shadow under his hat brim.

'If those idiots don't kill Farrington tonight, I'll do it myself. One thing's for sure: that peckerwood ain't coming back alive.'

Stanton followed on behind the vigilantes.

Farrington gave his horse its head and ran full tilt down the trail. He glanced over his shoulder and in the distance, he saw the dust cloud raised by the posse. Running the horse up the hillside, he looked back and Powder River spilled out in a shower of light across the valley floor. Farrington felt confident he could outrun them, he glanced up at the moon, it was so big he felt he could reach up and touch it. His laughter rolled across the night land and then he howled a coyote challenge. Unexpectedly, his horse stumbled and he heard its heavy laboured breathing and realized the horse was a soft horse, only fit for buzzard bait. He would not outrun anyone tonight.

The plains stood empty and barren but ahead on the right, a clump of trees in a fold in the land seemed the only feature in the emptiness. He headed down towards it as clouds tumbled across the moon. When he arrived at the tree line, he heard the thrum of the posse not far behind him and knew he had to fight his way out. He dragged the horse into cover, the night seemed alive with sound from the breeze in the undergrowth as it swept through the leaves and his breathing as he stood and waited. He had nowhere else to go, he would take it to them.

Six riders dragged on their horses' reins and pulled up in a flurry of dusty noise. Stanton reined in behind them and scanned the shadows. They all saw the shape of a man move through a patch of moonlight as Farrington walked out and stood in front of them.

'Well, you're here, boys. I don't reckon skulking in the shadows is my way at all.' He drew his gun and held it down the side of his leg. 'Looks like some of us will be having a drink in hell tonight.'

'Wait,' shouted Stanton and he held his hand up. The posse all quieted down at once, they knew Stanton's reputation as a hard man and a killer. Stanton dismounted and walked forward, his huge shadow fell across the clearing and stretched towards the smaller man like David and Goliath in the moonlight.

The moon looked cool and white like a lump of ice; Stanton bathed in its chill light like a shiver looking for a spine to run down.

'Farrington, I figure it's me against you and the winner walks away. What do you say? You're in a fine mess otherwise.'

'I've been in a lot worse. I tell you now, though, folk thought me bad before but when I get out of this, I'll let them know what bad means. But I do reckon you got yourself a deal. When I done beat you, I walk away, right?' As he spoke, Farrington raised his gun at Stanton.

The locals said later in the saloon that it was the fastest any of them had ever seen a man and gun move. As Farrington raised his arm, Stanton stood with his own gun holstered but he drew and threw off three shots and had it back in the holster before Farrington had time to level his gun.

Stanton's first shot hit Farrington high in the chest, the other two were wild and wide, racing into the trees. The impact made Farrington stagger back and he folded against a tree trunk, his gun still clutched in his dead hand. He dropped down dead without even realizing that Stanton had drawn and fired. Someone whistled and said, 'I reckon that boy's as dead as a can of corned beef.'

Stanton turned and said, 'Get him back to town.' He mounted up and cantered off.

The moonlight broke through the trees on the ridge and cast a silver light across the grass and leaves, and the breeze ruffled Farrington's hair.

One of the vigilantes nudged his horse forward and picked a rope from the side of his saddle horn. They roped Farrington's body by the feet and dragged him back to town. His back scoured the trail and his head bounced and nodded at the sky. His chest glistened redly.

Eugene Farrington wanted to make a name for himself but folk only remembered him as the little feller that Ned Stanton cleaned out good and proper.

12

Stanton turned up at Marshal Marcello's office early the next morning and told him what had happened the previous night.

'I heard some of it when they brought Farrington's body back,' said Marcello. 'There's no problem with you killing Farrington. They all witnessed how he threw a gun on you so that's all squared off. The body's at the undertakers with his brother.'

Marcello remembered the fear that gripped him when Farrington threatened him and said, 'Was Farrington any good with the gun?'

'You're only good if you kill the other feller. Killing folk is easier than it should be, I reckon. Now you report to that goddamn Sheriff Leeming today, tell him his escaped killer Farrington is dead.'

'Yes,' said Marcello, 'that means that Leeming has no reason to stay, he should leave town.'

Stanton nodded and said, 'You finally cottoned on, Marcello.' His eyes never left Marcello's face.

Marcello felt uncomfortable with Stanton's cold eyes sizing him up, he rubbed his cheek with the palm of his hand and it made a dry rasp across the stubble on his jaw, and he waited for Stanton to speak.

'Now we kill Jarrett,' said Stanton. 'He wants us to pay him off, I say we do it with a bullet.'

'You're right,' said Marcello. 'The only thing that ties us to the killing of old man Heggarty is Jarrett. Once he's dead we can walk away from it. We still need that Heggarty land.'

'One step at a time,' said Stanton.

★ ★ ★

While they talked in the jail, Heggarty went to find Sheriff Leeming. He was laid up in the same hotel while the local doctor patched him up.

The doctor took off his bowler hat and suit jacket. He wore black garters on his sleeves, he had a friendly face and a head as bald as a skinned onion. He fixed fresh bandages on Leeming's stump and the sheriff strapped on his wooden leg, stood and pulled up his baggy corduroy trousers and stamped his foot. 'Good as new,' he said. 'Thanks, Doc.' He pulled on his gun rig but felt the energy drain out of him like a balloon going down and he sagged back into an old armchair by the window. He scrapped the bowl of his pipe out with a knife, blew down the stem, pressed tobacco down into the bowl with his thumb, lit up and sat with his head wreathed in smoke.

Heggarty told him that Farrington was dead and that Stanton killed him.

The doctor packed away his case and looked up, his pale blinking eyes as big as an owl behind his glasses. He said, 'Stanton's a mystery, he's no rancher or farmer. He arrived in the last year and the small farmers hereabouts started giving up and moving on. The rumours are that Stanton forces them off the land or gets it cheap. The whole town's scared of him and so whatever land he wants, he seems to get.' He clicked his bag closed and turned towards them. 'That place he lives in belonged to the Barlow family and I treated Barlow before he left. He'd been beaten, three broken ribs and a snapped arm, I think he'd been gun whipped by the look of his face. He wouldn't say how it happened but he upped and left with his family a couple of days later. Stanton moved in but I hear that he's done nothing with the land or cabin.'

'I bet Jarrett was Stanton's lawyer,' said Sheriff Leeming, with his pipe stem clenched in his teeth.

'I believe he was,' said the doctor. 'Stanton certainly spent time in his company.'

After the doctor left Heggarty said, 'My pa's land borders the land where Stanton lives now.' He chewed on his finger, lost in thought. 'Stanton forces folk out and buys the land, uses Jarrett for the legal stuff then my pa's killed. Maybe it wasn't a robbery, maybe they wanted his land.'

'Would your father have sold out?' asked Leeming. 'Never. He'd put his life into that land.' He paused, realizing what he had said. 'You know what I mean. He wouldn't sell out even though he was getting past it.'

Leeming watched his pipe smoke hanging in the air. He leaned back in his chair and looked at Heggarty for a long time before he spoke.

'It looks as though Stanton tried to get his land and ended up killing him and made it seem like a robbery. Maybe anyway.'

'Yes, it all fits,' Heggarty said.

Sheriff Leeming shrugged his shoulders and said, 'Your ma's in a heap of trouble if you're right, I guess they still want the land. What are you figuring on doing, son?'

'I'm going to see the town marshal, he's called Marcello,' said Heggarty. He pushed himself away from the wall with his shoulders. 'You'll be leaving then, Sheriff?' he added, looking at Leeming.

'I have to,' said Leeming, tapping his pipe bowl out against his boot heel. 'Farrington's dead, I'm jiggered and I've no real authority hereabouts without the backing of a Federal Marshal. I'd say the town marshal's your best hope.'

'I must find Jarrett. He's the key to this, I bet if I put pressure on him he'll spill the beans about who killed my pa,' said Heggarty. He blew out his breath and scratched his head through his hat. 'There's Ahiga as well, maybe he can help me. He's still out there looking for Jarrett, I guess.'

'He's going to kill Jarrett as I recall.'
'Probably.'

'Listen,' said Leeming, leaning forward and resting his hands on his knees, 'I'll call on your ma and maybe stay a day or two and watch over her, nobody needs to know that, right?' He winked.

'Thanks, that's mighty fine of you. I appreciate any help,' said Heggarty. 'I'll keep it under my hat.'

Heggarty left and crossed the street to the town marshal's office. Marshal Marcello looked up from his desk when Heggarty came in.

'Can I help you?' said Marcello, studying Heggarty. 'I'm Sam Heggarty, someone gunned my pa, Walt Heggarty, a few days ago and I'm looking to put things right.'

Marcello swallowed hard, tasting pennies, then he coughed with a dry clicking sound as if his tongue stuck to the roof of his mouth. He said, 'I've been here over three years now, I knew your pa and liked him, he was a salty old boy,' said Marcello, trying hard to smile. He took out the makings and rolled himself a cigarette and let the smoke drift out of his mouth while he thought. Heggarty said, 'They brought Eugene Farrington's body in last night, I hear. I caught him and handed him in yesterday. He escaped from your cell. How did Farrington get a gun, sir?'

'Don't know. Maybe my deputy didn't shake him down too well but he paid for it right proper. He won't make that mistake again.'

'And my pa? Who killed him?'

'I'm working on it, son. It's a small town and I'm on my own now until I get me another deputy. It looks like robbery and murder. We got a local attorney called Buford Jarrett who ran off the night your pa was murdered. I reckon he's our killer,' said Marcello, squinting through the cigarette smoke.

'Buford Jarrett? I was on the stage when he high tailed it with Farrington.'

'You got it, that man Jarrett's a heap of trouble, ain't he?'

Heggarty said, 'I've got to get hold of Jarrett, I think he'll lead us to the killers.'

'Whoa, killers you say but it surely looks like Jarrett did it himself, don't it?'

Heggarty took a deep breath and said, 'We don't know until we find him, Marshal. He told Farrington that he could double the money in the bag. That sounds like the killing involved others and he could make them pay.'

'Does it? Or is it Jarrett backed into a

corner and trying hard to use Farrington to get out of it? He could have just lied to him and said anything to save his skin,' said Marcello in a reasonable tone. 'It worked anyway because Farrington's dead, Jarrett's free and this bag ain't turned up yet, either.'

Heggarty leaned forward, resting his hands on the marshal's desk.

'Will you help me find Jarrett?' he said, an edge of frustration creeping into his voice.

'I said I'm working hard on it, mister,' grunted Marcello, mashing out his cigarette. 'I've to bury my deputy right and proper first.'

'Then I won't keep you, Marshal.' Heggarty turned to leave but he hesitated and swung back to the marshal. 'What about Stanton?'

'What about Stanton?' said Marcello. He clasped his hands across his keg of a stomach, leaned back in his chair and tried to look casual.

'Stanton killed Farrington real quick. He's buying up land and sitting on it. He used Jarrett in those deals. He's deadly with his gun, maybe he killed my pa.'

Marshal Marcello puffed out his cheeks, looked hard at Heggarty and said, 'My, you surely have some thoughts spinning in that head of yours. Slow down, mister, get your grits off the stove. Don't you go pitching a fit. I'll talk to Stanton but there's no law against buying land and he killed an outlaw that stood pointing a gun at his belly. Plus, and hear this good, he played Faro in the saloon the night your pa was killed, he does that every goddamn night. You keep away from him, boy. You can't go accusing someone like him of murder unless you can show it's true and back it up. You're digging a hole for yourself, make sure it ain't a grave.'

13

Across country, Ahiga left the hidden cave and cantered over the hills with Jarrett's bag tied across his pony's rump and his brother's bow looped over his back.

Buford Jarrett turned and looked back over his shoulder. His arms were tied behind him, his wrists rubbed raw and bleeding and his legs tied together under his horse's chest. The rope around his neck trailed back to Ahiga who followed his prisoner to Powder River. Ahiga remembered his friend Heggarty's plea and decided that his revenge could wait. He gave his brother's killer his life back, for now. He knew that one way or another it would all end in Jarrett's death.

They rode in silence for an hour or more until Jarrett made a move. He thudded his boots into the horse's belly and tried to gallop off; the horse surged forward but the rope tightened around his neck and Ahiga held on and followed him. Jarrett's horse rushed across a ridge and clattered up a dry creek bed.

A shot rang out and startled them both. Two men rode in hard towards them, they shouted and then opened up with their guns, firing wildly in the air as they closed in. Ahiga had no choice but to let Jarrett go, swing his horse away and gallop off.

The two riders pulled up when they got to Jarrett, the older one said, 'What the hell you doing, pilgrim, letting a durned Indian rope you like a mule?'

The other rider holstered his gun and watched Ahiga ride off.

'Hey, Pa, look at that devil ride, he's faster than a skinned cat.' He looked about forty years old and wore a battered and patched old slouch hat on the back of his head. He had red hair and an angular face with big teeth and skin that you could strike a match on. He looked across at his father.

His father had a big chin, short black hair and skin so dark with sun and years of dirt that it looked like somebody had smoked him over an open fire. Even in the heat of the day, he wore an ancient full-length duster coat buttoned to the neck, which looked older than his son.

'I'm Albert Pugh, that's my boy Elijah.'

'Thank you for your help,' rasped Jarrett. His lips quivered and his pouchy face sagged like a wet paper bag.

Pugh looked at Jarrett slyly.

'Don't be too quick with the thanks, friend, unless you can back it up with a little money.' He rubbed his fingers down his thumb. 'Fair's fair, us helping out will cost you,' he said. He wheezed with pleasure and cackled with phlegmy laughter, grabbed the rope around Jarrett's neck and yanked on it hard. 'Cut him down, Eli, let's have a looksee at what we got. He looks fat enough for roasting. I reckon he's richer than possum gravy.'

Elijah walked over to Jarrett, drew a huge knife with a wicked looking blade and sliced through the rope on Jarrett's ankles, pushed him off the horse onto the ground and said, 'Come on, mister, empty your pockets.'

'Jesus H Christ, Elijah, his goddamn hands are tied. Break him out, I'll cover him.'

Elijah cut him loose and backed off and Jarrett showed them his pockets were empty and then to their astonishment, he turned and ran up the hill, scrabbling over rocks on his hands and knees. Albert laughed out loud.

'Go on, boy, git,' he shouted. 'Look at that, Eli, he's crazier than a trampled jack rabbit.'

'What do we do, Pa?'

'Let him run if that's what he wants. We'll leave him be, son, he can find his own way to hell.'

'He left his horse.'

'That's mighty generous of him, Eli, ain't it, it looks like he's paid us after all. I've a feeling this is going to be our lucky week.' As he spoke, the sun went behind a cloud and the cold went through him like an icicle.

14

Stanton sat at his plank table cleaning a gun, a nickel-plated Smith and Wesson with rosewood grips. He swabbed the bore with hot water and dried it before oiling it with deer tallow inside and out while he sat in a line of dirty sunlight that fell across the table. The wood of the inlaid handle was blackened with age but lined and patterned to help his grip. The front sights were filed down low so that it did not catch when he drew it. He took his time thumbing the cartridges in, spun the cylinder and watched the thick round base of each cartridge tick by one at a time. He slid the revolver into his holster, loaded his cartridge belt and buckled the full rig on as he stood, stretched his back and shoulders and enjoyed the weight of the gun knocking on his hip.

He heard a horse outside and without hurrying, he moved to the front window. The rider worked the horse down the incline with his knees. He rested his hands on the saddle horn, swaying with the motion of the horse.

Stanton walked out onto the veranda, brushing a fly out of his face.

'Ned Stanton, is that you?' said a familiar voice from his past.

'Cecil Moon as I live and breathe. What in tarnation are you doing in this neck of the woods?' Stanton called from the shadows and stepped out into the sunlight.

'Come to see you, cousin, heard you was up in these parts, asked for you at the saloon and they pointed me in this direction,' said Moon. He was about twenty years old, if you believed the wanted posters, but he looked older with dark hair, a thin hatchet face, pock-marked skin and cruel eyes. He wore a striped flannel shirt, shabby canvas trousers and a wide leather belt high on his waist.

'You're on the run then,' said Stanton.

'Well, something like. They're saying I killed three men for double-crossing me.

It ain't true. I only killed two and one of them definitely deserved it. I need to cool my heels a while, I could surely use a friendly face, somewhere to stay and some money, in that order.'

'Inside,' said Stanton and he turned and went back into the cabin.

Moon walked in like he owned the place and crossed to the stove. He felt the coffee pot and poured himself a cup. His flat savage eyes smouldered with a grudge against the world.

'There's nothing for you here, Cecil, I've got a nice piece of action that's almost played out, you just keep your nose out of my hog trough. And stay out of sight, I don't want you being recognized or causing trouble.'

'Now that's not proper, us being kin an' all,' said Moon, watching Stanton's face but there was nothing to read there, his expression looked dead of all emotion; it was like looking in an empty cupboard.

They both turned to the window when they heard a horse being ridden full tilt down the slope.

'Someone's trying right hard to run the hoofs off that horse,' said Moon.

'I hope you weren't followed in, Cecil, are you getting careless? Stay put. And don't kill nobody.'

Without waiting for an answer, Stanton crossed to the front of the cabin, stepped outside and jerked the door shut behind him.

Heggarty hauled his horse up hard, clouding up red dirt off a track that led back to the barn where Moon's mount, a muscular jet black quarter horse, stood snuffing and blowing by the water trough. Heggarty stood up in his stirrups, pointed at Stanton and said, 'You've got some explaining to do, mister.'

'Don't point at me, boy, or I'll snap your finger off,' said Stanton. He stood relaxed, his voice low but with a hard edge to it, and his eyes like slits in his grim face. 'State your piece and get gone.'

'I will. I'm not staying but I'm on to you, sir. The jig's up, I reckon you killed my pa. I'll find your attorney Jarrett and when I do, I'll be back, that I do promise,' said Heggarty and with that, he heeled his horse in the belly and thundered back up the trail, raising a screen of dust that followed him over the ridge.

'Right friendly neighbours,' said Moon from the now open doorway. 'That fool's running round like a hornet doused in hot water.' He turned and went back inside.

Out of sight, Heggarty slowed his horse, pushed his hat back on his head and smiled to himself. He hoped that little show would rattle Stanton and make him do something careless. He'd kicked the hog pen and hoped it stirred up a stink. He wanted Stanton angry and feeling threatened so that he'd rush things and make a mistake. He learned to be patient from breaking horses but goddamn it, he thought, sometimes you've got to poke it with a stick and meet it face to face.

He made to head back to Powder River but as he looked across the valley, he saw windswept grass on jumbled hills crisped to a fine summer gold and watched a herd of wild running mustang flow like liquid down a ridge. He missed home and his family but felt he had a duty to his father to find the men who killed him. Best keep busy, he thought, so he decided to scout the land for signs of Jarrett while he waited for Stanton's next move.

The doctor told them that Stanton bought other small holdings so Heggarty figured the land lay idle. There would be abandoned buildings where Jarrett could hide out. He decided to have a look around. He pushed on with the tall grass whipping under his horse's chest, unaware that Stanton had already made his move.

As Heggarty rode away, Stanton went back inside and watched Moon eating cold beans from a tin with his knife.

'Trouble then,' said Moon with his mouth full of food. 'I guess maybe you can use some help.'

'It's nothing I cain't handle, Cecil, you know that,' said Stanton. He watched

Moon eating while he turned things over in his mind. 'Still and all,' he said after a while, 'I can put some work your way.'

'As long as it pays.'

'You get what I give you. Don't get comfortable. Did you see the lunkhead outside shooting his mouth off?' said Stanton.

Moon nodded, licked his knife clean and said, 'Well, I saw his horse better, one of those paint horses, wasn't it, dark with white patterning down the chest and forelegs. Rider wore a blue coat and black hat.'

Stanton took a roll of notes from his pocket and counted some out.

'Here's near enough fifty bucks. I want you to ride out yonder and plug that boy good. Kill him and leave the body on the edge of town. I'll go into town now so folks can see it wasn't my doing.'

Moon rubbed his hand down the side of his trousers and held out his hand for the money. He stood, hitched his belt up and as he left he said, 'That peck-erwood's as good as dead. See you again, cousin,' and he walked out with a strut that reeked of violence.

Moon decided to follow Heggarty and let Stanton get to town, so he could make a quick kill, dump the body and move on before the dust settled.

He stopped on the ridge where the valley swept away between low hills on either side, forming a chute of land and he could see Heggarty in the distance.

Moon whipped his reins across the horse's shoulder and raced across the pasture up to the timberline. He stopped on the top of the bluff in the dappled shade of the trees and below, saw Heggarty walk his horse down a track towards a cabin. The land around the cabin was part rail fenced and tilled in dark rectangles at the back but there were no signs that the sodbuster who worked the holding still lived there.

He watched Heggarty dismount and walk to a shack with his rifle in his hand. He vanished around the far side, wandered back out and checked the lean-to, remounted and rode back to the track and cantered off to the east.

Moon followed hugging the side of the slope, as he crested a butte he dragged on the reins. Heggarty sat on his horse with his back to him only a hundred paces or so below him, and drank from his canteen and studied another cabin set back down a weed-choked track. Moon watched Heggarty finish his drink, draw his rifle and nudge his horse down the path to the shack.

He pulled his own horse back into the shadows of the rocks and crept forward with his rifle. He hunkered down next to a bush, lay down and brought his rifle to his shoulder and made ready for his shot. He said to himself, 'I guess you're looking for someone or something, friend, but it don't look like you'll find it there. I reckon you'll be back up that track right soon and step nice and clear into my sights when you do.'

He wriggled down to get more comfortable, blinked the sweat from his eyes and levered a cartridge into the breech.

'This is as easy as licking butter off a

knife. Come to Cecil,' he said.

As Moon watched him, Heggarty got to the abandoned shack, next to it stood a small well and a pasture that ran down the side of the cabin. Heggarty looked around the yard, an empty railed pen and a bladeless rotting small windmill strung with dead brush blown across from a field of weeds. The rain moved in quickly out of the north, dimming the fields and clicking on his jacket and hat. It fell like a wet curtain and made it difficult to see or hear anything. He walked through pools of rain water and rubbed his thumb down his cheek where the rain from his hat brim dripped in his face.

He pushed on the shack door but it would not move, he put his shoulder to it and threw his weight against it. The bottom of the door scraped across the buckled floorboards then freed itself and flew open. Heggarty half stumbled inside but before he could straighten up a rock walloped him on the back of the head.

Heggarty was out cold when Jarrett rolled him over. Jarrett recognized him from the stage as the man who helped the Indian. He pulled off Heggarty's jacket and went through the pockets, taking the money he found there. He threw the jacket down but picked it up again and put it on. His own coat and hat were back in the cave. He snatched Heggarty's hat from the ground and jammed it down on his head and rushed outside for the horse. He could not believe his luck, his problems were over, he was free.

He splashed through the ground water in the pouring rain, got on the horse, slapped it hard and galloped off down the track.

Ahead of him Moon smiled.

'I knew it, you got the wrong pig by the tail when you riled my family.' He fixed the iron sights squarely on the rider's head, squeezed the trigger and watched his body catapult off the back of the horse like he had been hit with an invisible club.

The shot roused Heggarty, he staggered to his feet, picked up his rifle and stepped outside.

The rain stopped suddenly and the darkness lifted as the sun broke through the cloud banks. Heggarty saw his horse standing by a broken fence pawing the ground. A body lay in a big rain puddle with blood trailing in the water like red smoke. He heard another horse riding down from the crag and he ducked down behind a mound of soil, levelled his rifle and waited.

Heggarty did not know Moon but he realized that he saw his dark quarter horse outside Stanton's cabin that morning. He watched Moon dismount and roll the body over with the toe of his boot. Heggarty stood and pointed his gun.

'Who are you?' he said.

Moon's head jerked up and his hand tightened on his rifle stock but he shrugged and said, 'Nobody you'd know, I killed this trash as a favour to a friend. I don't know who you are but this is my business and you should be proper glad to keep it that way.'

'Did Stanton send you? I'm sure I saw

your horse at his place earlier.'

Moon realized he had shot the wrong man but the surprise did not show on his face, it looked as calm and still as deep water. His eyes did not stray or blink, they locked on Heggarty's face and stayed there.

'I don't know no Stanton but I did get some chow from a man this morning, right neighbourly, maybe our paths crossed. I don't think you should point that gun at me while we're talking neither.' Heggarty lowered the rifle a little and started down the track towards him.

'So who've you shot?' said Heggarty.

'He just cracked my head and stole my coat and horse.'

'You should be pleased I plugged him then.' As Moon spoke he slid his rifle back in the saddle holster. 'See, I ain't got a problem with you, I'm going to mount up and get gone.'

He slipped his boot in the stirrup and pulled himself up, drew his handgun and held it against his horse's neck on the side away from Heggarty. As he sat he brought the gun out and snapped off a shot. Heggarty felt the pull of the bullet as it tugged at his shirt collar and thudded into a fence post behind him. A second shot followed and nicked him, flicking a thread of blood across his neck. Heggarty fired and saw his bullet hit Moon high in the chest with a thump that rocked him in his saddle as his gun fell from his lifeless hand.

He pitched forward into the puddle on top of Jarrett's body. Heggarty walked over and as he got closer, he realized that the first body was Jarrett. Moon's bullet had hit him high in the head and shattered his face. Despair welled up in Heggarty's throat, his face grey and still he stared down at the body and realized that whatever Jarrett knew about his father's death had just died with him.

He heard a horse ride down and looked up to see Ahiga slide from its back. Ahiga knelt by Jarrett's head, looked at the tattered skull, turned to Heggarty and said, 'The Great Spirit protects my brother. This man will know no peace in the spirit world now his eyes are gone. My revenge is over.' He stood up. 'I will help you, my friend. I have the bag you wanted.'

'Thank you, Ahiga, my friend.' They clasped each other's arm, wrist to wrist. 'You've brought me hope just when I needed it most. I'm glad your revenge is over,' said Heggarty, smiling. 'My revenge ain't even started yet.'

15

Stanton sat at the oval Faro table with four others and the dealer. Stanton felt in a good mood, he figured his cousin Cecil Moon had killed Heggarty by now and the cards were working for him. There were raised voices over at the bar and the drinkers there started to crowd the windows and spill out onto the street. The game stopped as the noise grew and the room emptied. The dealer called over to one of the doves.

'What's happening, Belle?'

A woman turned from the window and said, 'They brought a body in, I think, over at the jail house.'

Stanton raised his eyes from the cards laid across the table and smiled.

'Hold the game,' said Stanton.

The dealer was amazed, Stanton had never spoken since the first night he joined in the game months ago. He swallowed at the memory of that night, he

145

used the dealing box to draw two cards at the same time and he looked up and saw Stanton stare at him with lidless reptile eyes.

Stanton said, 'A pair of six shooters beats a two card draw.' The dealer slipped one card back in the box and continued the game but swore he would never cheat again, at least when Stanton was at the table. So when Stanton said hold the game the game stopped.

'I'll be back, don't move anything,' said Stanton and he knew no-one would.

There were two horses tied to the rail outside the jail as Stanton shoved his way through the crowd. He saw the backside of a body laid across a horse and he grinned but his jaw went rigid with anger when he saw it was Moon's horse and body. Stanton stood grim-faced, looking as if he was chewing broken glass. He pulled out a cigar and clenched it in his teeth without lighting it, trying hard to hide his anger.

'The other one's that attorney Jarrett,' someone said and Stanton noticed the body laid on the sidewalk. He thumbed a match alight and lit his cigar, letting the smoke roll out of his nose, then turned and walked back to the saloon. His anger turned to satisfaction as he thought it through. Jarrett was dead so the witness was gone, the killing of his no account cousin Moon was a price worth paying for that. He remembered the money he gave Moon that morning and reminded himself to tell Marcello that he wanted it back.

He went back to the bar and ordered bourbon, sat down and told them to restart the Faro game.

Across the street, Marshal Marcello sat at his desk, County Sheriff Leeming perched on the corner of the table and Heggarty leaned against the wall.

'Explain again,' said Marcello, looking at Heggarty. 'I told you once, I was out looking for Jarrett. He jumped me and stole my horse, the stranger shot him as he rode away. I came out and he tried to shoot me and I killed him.'

'Why did this stranger kill Jarrett and

try to kill you?' said Marcello.

'Ask him,' snapped Heggarty, 'I don't know.'

The room reeked of kerosene and heat from the lamp and the potbellied stove in the corner. Heggarty struggled to stay calm.

'Did anyone else see what happened?' asked Marcello.

'No one else was about.' Heggarty sighed. 'I told you that.'

'And Jarrett said nothing?'

'No, goddamn it, he was deader than dead when I got to him.'

'And this stranger just upped and shot at you,' said Marcello, chewing on the corner of his moustache. 'You say you don't know him?'

'No, I don't know him,' said Heggarty truthfully but he decided not to mention seeing the horse at Stanton's or bring Ahiga into it, some instinct told him not to trust Marcello.

'Well, Heggarty,' said Marcello, 'we'll never know no more than that I guess.' He looked at Sheriff Leeming and added,

'I'm thinking this — tell me I'm wrong — Jarrett killed Heggarty's pa. Then he runs off. Then someone kills Jarrett. So it's all over and done with.' Marcello studied his hands on the desktop.

'There ain't anywhere else to look and no-one else to look for.'

Heggarty pushed himself off the wall and went out of the door without speaking, his mouth a grim line as he fought to control his temper. Leeming raised his eyebrows and followed Heggarty outside.

'Have you eaten yet?' said Sheriff Leeming as they came out of the marshal's office.

Heggarty shook his head and they went down the street to an eating house and ordered plates of spicy sausage, beans and fried potatoes.

'It doesn't wash,' said Heggarty, playing with his food. 'Stanton's mixed up in this and Marshal Marcello is either crooked or a bonehead, I believe he knows more than he's letting on.'

Sheriff Leeming spoke through a

149

mouthful of food. 'You can bet on it. Are you eating the rest of that sausage?'

Heggarty pushed his plate across the table and Leeming forked the food into his mouth.

'I didn't tell Marcello this but Ahiga got Jarrett's bag and gave it to me,' said Heggarty. 'I haven't looked in it properly yet, I left it with Ahiga outside town.'

'I knew it,' said Leeming. 'I could tell you were holding something back. Who was the stranger you killed? I don't think Marcello knew him. But I tell you what I think for nothing — he meant to kill you, not Jarrett. He waited for you to ride out and Jarrett had your horse and your clothes, I think he was set to kill you. I cain't figure why.'

'I riled Stanton earlier in the day and I saw that stranger's horse outside of Stanton's place while I was there. I tried to make Stanton show his hand and I think it played out from there.'

'Yes,' said Leeming, 'you sure stomped on a rattler's tail there, son. Come on, let's get gone. We'll go to your ma and have a looksee in that bag. I'll tell Marcello I'm done here and I'm heading back to Owl Creek. That way he'll figure it's all squared away and he can lock the barn door on it. The less he knows the better. I reckon we'll be bumping into him again down the line. When we find out who killed your old man, you just remember to go in hard, shoot straight and pull all of them down.'

'Count on it.'

★ ★ ★

Heggarty, Ahiga and Sheriff Leeming met up outside town, cut through the trees and poured it on down the valley, riding hard the forty miles or so to the Heggarty place. They came down off the steep sided thickly wooded hills. The Heggarty cabin had a barn, a railed corral and crops on three sides with a brown creek running alongside.

Heggarty sat for an hour talking with his mother and handed over the bits of jewellery from the bag. Hannah Heggarty was a handsome woman, about fifty years old with long dark hair streaked with grey. She had large green eyes and a clear complexion. She wore a long sleeved plain cream blouse and an ankle length blue skirt. She played with the brooch, sighed and closed her hand around it. She looked up at Heggarty and smiled.

'How are Mary and the boys?'

'They're fine, Ma. You come see us as soon as I sort this out. I asked you to come live with us a year or so ago, remember, but Pa wouldn't leave this place.' Heggarty held up his hand. 'I understand why he did it, Ma, don't worry. But I'd like you to think about it again now.'

'I will, Sam. I wish you'd go back now but I know you feel you have to get some justice for your pa.'

Heggarty nodded and put his hand over his mother's and said, 'You've got to look out for your own.'

Mrs Heggarty agreed, she busied herself making everyone welcome and cooked scrambled eggs, grits, fried fatback and cornbread. While they were eating, she said, 'You know, Sam, you need to talk to Albert and Elijah Pugh. They often rummage around here after dark. Your pa let them help themselves to a few potatoes, grain and the like. He'd have given them some straight up if they'd asked but they liked to come in and take it when they thought he wasn't looking. I bet they were around on the night your pa was killed, maybe they saw something.'

'I don't know them, they must have arrived after I went south.' Heggarty's mother nodded. 'Come on, Ahiga, let's go talk to them salty old birds, maybe they saw something the night Pa died.'

Leeming said, 'I'll stay and keep your ma company.' He looked at Heggarty, they both knew she needed protection. 'I'll study those papers in the bag you brought as well. I doubt there's much going to happen here tonight.'

Heggarty and Ahiga rode off, following Mrs Heggarty's directions until below them the river surface lay like black metal in the dark valley bottom. 'Over there,' Ahiga said. 'Where rocks are, they live there. We go round back and come behind them.' 'I will talk to them, Ahiga,' said Heggarty.

'I watch, I have seen these men before, they do not like Shoshone,' said Ahiga, his dark face unreadable.

They looked down on a crude wood-framed sod shack with a low roof of crumbling cedar logs covered in an old blackened tarp, no windows and a door opening covered with a blanket.

Two mules and a horse were hobbled in front of the shack in an area choked with undergrowth and littered with lumps of rotting lumber, old wheels and horse dung. A fire glowed in a small pit. Heggarty walked down.

'Hello Mr Pugh, I'm Sam Heggarty. My pa was Walter Heggarty. I need your help.' One of the horses looked up at him and he heard scuffling and cursing inside the shack.

A rifle barrel pushed aside the blanket from inside.

154

'State your business,' said a voice.

'I guess you and your son know my pa was killed,' Heggarty said. He gambled that they were around that night and continued. 'I know you were about on the night he died and I'd like to know if you saw who killed him. I brought some whiskey for you, let's drink it out here.' He held out a pint bottle.

Albert stepped out, bringing with him an eye-watering smell like a tanner's yard on a hot day; the smell covered Heggarty's face like a wet cloth. Albert's chest wheezed like a blocked chimney.

'Right friendly of you, neighbour,' he said, propping his rifle against the wall and taking the bottle. He pulled the cork with his teeth and spat it aside, tipped the bottle and took a long swig, smacking his lips as he finished.

'My, that's mighty fine drinking whiskey,' he said and took another slow pull. A taller, younger man stepped out behind him.

'Come on, Pa, let me try some,' he said. 'Here you are, mister, you have some of ours.' He held out a jug towards Heggarty. 'This mash will hit you right between the eyes.'

Heggarty took it and pretended to take a mouthful. He felt it burn his lips and the smell hammered at his nose and squeezed his throat, making him cough.

Albert threw a rotted hunk of ponderosa wood onto the fire and stepped back from the flames and heat as the sparks showered upwards and blew across his legs. His face was lit red by the fire and the drink. He said, 'I like your ma and pa. I'll tell you what we saw. And you tell your ma I'll be over to see if she needs any help. That's an Albert Pugh promise. Anyway we were there right enough when your pa was killed. We heard it and saw them ride off. I said to Elijah,' continued Albert, nodding towards his son, 'we need to save our own bacon and get gone right sharp or they'll be cooking us next. So we got to hell and gone down the road.'

'You saw them then?'

'Yes, I done told you. Well, the first

one out we didn't rightly see, a little fat man scuttled out like his tail was afire and rode off in a buggy. But we knew the other two all right. I told my boy we say nothing, we don't want no trouble.'

Albert looked at Heggarty and said, 'Stanton, he was one of them. I'd keep well clear of him, anything I done bad he's done it twice over.'

'I guessed he'd be in on it,' said Heggarty. 'Albert, I need the name of the other man and a promise you tell Marshal Marcello who you saw.'

Albert looked at Elijah and they laughed.

'No, boy, I won't promise to tell Marcello,' Albert said 'Seeing as how he already knows, you see, he was the other feller who killed your pa.'

16

Marshal Marcello met Stanton at Stanton's cabin, unaware that Heggarty was talking to the Pughs. Marcello said, 'So who was the dead body they brought in? The feller that killed Jarrett, you knew him, didn't you? Tell me I'm wrong.'

'He was my kin, Cecil Moon, I paid him to kill Heggarty.'

'And a fine job he made of it,' said Marcello. His neck flushed with anger, his heavy face set, his cheeks flecked with small blue and red veins as he looked at Stanton from under his hat brim.

Stanton turned slowly and glared at Marcello, his eyes level and unblinking, like he was measuring him for a coffin. Marcello realized he had almost gone too far, he knew that it wasn't just what Stanton had said that frightened him, it was the silence afterwards that made it worse. Stanton said, 'I told him nothing. There's no connection between me and him hereabouts. Heggarty came blustering in shooting his mouth off, I would've killed him myself but I was trying to keep clear of that pleasure for now, that's all. Cecil had just arrived, said he'd do the job and move on.'

'Did Heggarty see him with you?'

'No. Cecil stayed inside,' said Stanton, then he thought for a moment. 'He might have seen his horse outside though.'

'I wouldn't bet against it,' said Marcello. 'He probably has a fair idea of what we've been up to. Let's figure on him knowing everything.'

Stanton took a slow drink of coffee and said, 'We both know that fat lawyer Jarrett was the real threat to us because of what he saw and knew and he's dead now.'

Marcello nodded and calmed himself; he did not want to push Stanton too far.

'Yes,' Marcello said, 'you're right. Hannah Heggarty is back so I say we take her and make her sign the land over.'

'And you reckon her son will just sit by and let us?'

159

'Yes, I do,' said Marcello. 'We take his ma tonight and hide her away. Then you go and find Heggarty and you tell him straight up that you'll kill her if he pokes his nose in. We want his family's land.'

Stanton nodded and Marcello felt a growing confidence. He said, 'We've got all the land that the Colonel asked us to get but for this bit the Heggartys hold. Once we've got that we're all done right dandy but we've got to move quick, I need this settling. If you want, you can kill them both after the deal's done.'

'Slow down, Marcello, stop stoking your own furnace,' said Stanton. 'Let's get the woman and take it from there.' Stanton smiled a cold, hard smile. 'I kill them, I like that real good.' He looked at Marcello with dark, deep watchful eyes filled with anger and cruelty.

'Let's get to the Heggarty place tonight and take the woman. Come on, let's do this thing,' said Marcello, heading for the door.

★ ★ ★

Night fell as Marcello and Stanton arrived at the Heggarty cabin.

A lamp glowed in the barn and they watched Hannah Heggarty close the barn door and walk to the cabin. They crept down to the creek and worked their way along its bank. The moon reflected on the water and looked to be trapped under the surface. The water gurgled and the trees rustled as they passed. The air felt cool and damp and smelt of wet earth. They did not notice or care.

Marcello dragged the barn door open and went inside to get a horse to carry Mrs Heggarty. He looped a bridle over the nearest one. The horse tossed its head and backed away. It kicked out with its back hoofs and thumped them against the barn wall with a hollow thud. Marcello grabbed a quirt from a rack and whipped it hard across the horse's shoulder.

'Git,' he said and the horse allowed itself to be dragged out of the stall.

'Sam, is that you?' Mrs Heggarty called from the cabin doorway as she dried her

161

hands on her apron.

Marcello stood stock still and waited, hoping Stanton would do something.

Mrs Heggarty started for the barn; behind her Stanton ran from the shadows and grabbed her. He put one arm around her throat and his other clamped her around the waist.

'Be quiet or I'll snap your neck right quick,' said Stanton in a hoarse whisper, his mouth so close to her ear that she felt his breath on her neck and smelled the tobacco on his clothes. He carried her easily to the barn door and threw her inside, where she rolled like a rag doll and cracked her head on a timber support post.

'Get her tied on the horse and get out of here, I'll cover you,' Stanton said to Marcello and he swung around and walked back into the yard. Behind him, two horses thundered out of the barn as Marcello dragged Mrs Heggarty and her horse behind him. Roused by the noise, Sheriff Leeming rushed out of the cabin, his hair tousled and his voice thick with sleep.

'Hannah, what in tarnation is going on out there? Who's that?' he shouted as the horses disappeared over the ridge. He stopped and leaned against the door jamb as pain flared up his bad leg, it felt like a dog was chewing at his knee. He saw Stanton over by the barn.

Stanton drew his gun, cocked the hammer in one fluid movement and said, 'Stay right where you are and keep those hands where I can see them.' He did not recognize Sheriff Leeming but would not have cared anyway.

Leeming tensed, ready to throw himself back inside the cabin but out of the corner of his eye he saw movement in the far shadows behind Stanton and realized that Sam Heggarty stood by the side of a pile of wooden boxes.

'I'm coming down, mister,' said Leeming to distract Stanton, 'but I've got a bad leg so you'll have to give me a minute.' He stepped out and his leg crumpled under him and he pitched forward. 'Looks like you'll have to help me up,' he said from the ground.

Stanton looked down at him and spat.

'The hell I will, mister, I'm … ' And then he heard the whisper of boots on the gravel behind him, he half turned as Heggarty ran in and hit him square in the back with his shoulder. Stanton lost his gun and he fell to his knees. Heggarty stood over him and kicked him hard in the ribs. Heggarty stepped back, raised his Spencer rifle and levered a bullet into the breech.

'Wait,' said Stanton, speaking in a level voice without fear. 'We've got your ma. If you kill me, you'll never see her again, that I promise.'

Leeming said, 'It looks like someone did just ride out of here with her, son.'

Heggarty nodded.

'I won't kill you yet, Stanton,' he said. 'You'll hang for killing my pa. Before that, I'm going to beat you good.' He shucked off his jacket, folded it with care and laid it on the ground. 'Get up, I'm minded to beat the hell out of you.'

Stanton smiled, stood, took off his

coat and threw it aside. His face looked to be carved out of oak, he had a thick neck corded with veins and wide sloping shoulders.

'Yes,' he said, 'that's a right good idea, let's see what you're made of.'

Stanton rolled his neck, he had the look of a man whose life was totally consumed in fury.

'You know, boy,' he said, 'you've been aching for a lesson since I first saw you and I'm the buck to give you one.' His size seemed to give off a heat and a threat of toughness and violence you could almost grab a hold of. Heggarty did not care, he rushed in and shot out his left fist but Stanton flicked it away easily. Heggarty instantly drove a hard right into Stanton's guts but hit a wall of muscle.

'My old man whupped me harder than that, boy,' said Stanton and he fired off a fast punch that caught Heggarty above the eye. Heggarty shook it off and tried to move around Stanton. They swapped a couple of jabs, hitting each other's arms and then Heggarty whipped off a good right that crunched Stanton's nose. Blood ran down his face but he just dropped back a step, hawked out a string of red saliva and moved back in.

'My nose is already mashed, you cain't harm it anymore.'

Stanton was a big man, a body puncher who took the pain in his powerful arms and kept his head behind his big fists. He stepped up close to work Heggarty over with a flurry of punches, jabbing into Heggarty's arms and ribs. Heggarty countered with a hammered hook to Stanton's jaw that made him blink and spit but did not stop him coming in. Stanton seemed happy to take pain as long as he could give more out. He had six inches in height and reach and thirty pounds in weight going for him.

Heggarty took another couple on the arms, ducked and pummelled Stanton's gut but he got a glancing blow to the side of his head that started to bleed.

'Felt that one didn't you, Heggarty?'

said Stanton with a short laugh and he threw two hard rights, the second one hit Heggarty's ribs and brought tears to his eyes. 'I'm going to finish you right soon, boy.'

Heggarty started weaving and bobbing from side to side but Stanton caught him on the top of the head, opening another cut; the blood ran down his face and he tasted it as it fell across his mouth. Stanton threw another punch Heggarty's way but he slipped it and drove two hard jabs into Stanton's ribs. He never saw the next one from Stanton as it clocked him above the jaw and the world jacked out of focus. Stanton moved in to finish him.

Heggarty drove up through the mist in his brain and hooked an uppercut on the underside of Stanton's chin, the punch so hard it all but lifted Stanton off his feet. Heggarty moved in with a left-right combination, forcing Stanton to back away but Heggarty followed him, raining punches in like a jack-hammer. Stanton leaned his back against the barn wall and Heggarty punched his body and face until Stanton slid to the ground and covered his head with his arms. Heggarty pulled Stanton's head up by his hair and spat in his face then let him slump to the ground.

'Hold it now, son,' shouted Leeming, 'we'll have to let him go.'

'I know,' said Heggarty. He stood back and cleaned the blood from his face with his shirt sleeve.

Leeming said, 'Remind me not to annoy you. You all but knocked him right into the middle of next week.' They both moved over and watched Stanton get to his feet.

Stanton stood, blew the blood out of his nose with his fingers and dabbed his mouth before running his tongue across his teeth.

'It ain't finished between the two of us, Heggarty, not by a long way. We have your ma and if you want to see her again, you'd best get out of my goddamn way.' Heggarty's face flushed with anger and he made to move forward but Sheriff Leeming put his hand on his shoulder and held him back.

'So what happens next?' said Leeming.

'Well, his ma is going to sign over this land to us,' said Stanton, his left eye swollen in a purple knot.

'You tell Marcello if he harms her, I'll hunt him down and gut him like a hog,' said Heggarty. He saw Stanton's surprise when he mentioned Marcello. 'Yes, I know you and him are in it up to your necks. And you'll swing before this is over.'

'Marcello?' said Stanton, trying to look puzzled. 'Yes, Marcello, I know you two killed my pa, I've found two folks who saw you do it.'

'They're dadburned liars whoever they are. I was in town and I'm sure Marcello will be able to tell anyone who wants to know what he was doing. I figure you're bluffing,' said Stanton.

'Get the hell out of here, Stanton. You get my ma and bring her back here tomorrow and make sure she's not hurt,' said Heggarty, his arms folded across his chest and his face tight with anger.

Stanton laughed, picked up his gun, and walked off to find his horse.

'I'm sorry they got to your ma,' said Leeming. 'I fell asleep. All I know is when I came out two horses rode off. I guess that was Marcello and your ma. Stanton was in the yard.'

'Yes, I heard a ruckus as we rode over. I left my horse with Ahiga and I snuck in,' said Heggarty, then he paused. 'It sure felt good thrashing Stanton.'

★   ★   ★

Stanton made his way to his own cabin. His arms and ribs felt sore and started to stiffen from the fight and his nose hurt like hell. He could feel the skin on his face pull as the blood dried in the night breeze.

As he walked into the cabin Marcello said, 'What the hell happened to you? You look like someone whipped your face with a piece of lumber.'

'Heggarty,' said Stanton. 'He jumped

me before I could get out. I figured it best to mess with him so that you could get gone. I gave as good as I got and delivered the message about his ma.'

'I've put her in the cellar, no-one will find her there. She ain't spoken but I think she came round and saw me, so she knows I'm involved.'

'So does her boy Heggarty,' said Stanton. 'He said he's got two folk who saw you there on the night we took out his pa.'

'Who saw us?' Marcello said as the blood drained from his face. His fingernails were bitten down low and his forehead ridged like a washboard.

'He didn't say, but I reckon we were seen,' said Stanton.

'I can't believe anyone was around at that time of night,' said Marcello. He lit a cigarette, lifted his head back and blew smoke towards the rafters while he thought. 'Why would anyone from town be skulking about out there after dark?' He dropped his cigarette on the floor and crushed it with his boot. 'Goddamn it, it'll be those Pughs. They're a couple of

171

poor white trash who scrounge and steal from the farms hereabouts. I reckon we need to pay those crackers a visit.'

'Looks to me like the gig's up here anyway, Marcello. One way or another, Heggarty's on to us for killing his pa. There was another man at the Heggarty place, I guess he knows everything as well. I ain't seen him before. Tall, mustache, fiftyish with a bad leg, said he was a county sheriff.'

Marcello slammed his palm down onto the table, making the cups jump. Stanton looked at him and raised his eyebrows.

Marcello said, 'Leeming, the County Sheriff out of Owl Creek. Now we got a whole load of grief. Still an' all, if we get the Heggarty land, we can get our money and leave before it all goes sour. Let's go see the Colonel tonight and tell him how things stand.'

'He won't like it. You shouldn't go there and he don't want to hear your problems, believe me,' said Stanton.

'He only needs to know what I tell

him. I'll say we'll be finished by tomorrow. We'll get the Heggarty land, take him the papers and he can pay us off. I'll tell him it's got a bit hot for us and we've got to scoot. We don't get paid until the last piece of land is signed over so we go tonight and tell him to have the money ready. When we've got the land, we go back over to the Colonel to drop off the paperwork, collect our dues and skedaddle,' said Marcello.

Stanton studied Marcello and decided to let him do what he wanted, all he could think about was settling the score with Heggarty, his humiliation at the beating burned in him like a match flame against his skin.

'One way or another, Heggarty's going to die,' said Stanton, staring off into the distance.

Outside the cabin, Albert Pugh and his son Elijah hunkered down in the undergrowth. Albert pulled a wad of tobacco out of his pocket, ignored the coating of dust and fluff and pushed it into his mouth.

Ten minutes later, Stanton and Marcello appeared, mounted up and rode off. Albert stood, his knees cracked and he spat a string of tobacco juice into the bushes.

'Elijah, we're going down yonder, bring the mules.'

'There's nothing worth taking, Pa, we already looked,' said Elijah.

'Whist, boy,' said Albert. 'I promised young Heggarty I'd watch out for his ma. We're going to do just that, we'll fetch Hannah out of there and get her home.'

In the stable they saw Mrs Heggarty's horse but no sign of her. Elijah stood by the door post scratching his armpit.

'They must have put her in the root cellar,' he said and both of them moved inside and kicked the rotting straw out of the way. Elijah grabbed a rusted floor ring and dragged a section of the floorboards to one side and Albert shuffled down the steps and disappeared from sight.

'She's down here right enough,' called

up Albert, his voice muffled by the darkness of the cellar. 'We're coming out.' He climbed out supporting Hannah Heggarty.

'Thank you, boys,' she said, brushing dust from her clothes. 'I'll be fine once I get moving and get out of this stink.'

'What stink?' said Elijah.

'You're a fine woman, Hannah,' murmured Albert. 'Me and Elijah will see you home. It's over. We're all safe now.'

17

While the Pughs pulled Mrs Heggarty free and started back, her son, Sam, and Sheriff Leeming sat at the kitchen table. The contents of the carpet bag lay out in front of them. Leeming puffed at his pipe and looked at the papers through a veil of tobacco smoke. He tapped the paper by his arm with the stem of his pipe.

'You see, son, Stanton ain't the land-owner after all, no, sir. This says the lands are all owned by one Colonel Lovell DeVere, he's the real rogue behind all of this. He must be using Stanton and Marcello to force folk off the land and then he gets it in his name.'

Heggarty nodded. Looking at a map from the bag spread across the table, he flattened and smoothed the map with his hand and ran his finger across it.

'They mark off everything and it looks like they bought a long strip of land for over a hundred miles, give or take. The one bit they don't have is our land right here,' said Heggarty.

Leeming sucked on his pipe and said, 'It's a cattle trail, is my guess. Have you heard of the Goodnight Loving cattle trail?' Heggarty nodded. 'It comes out of Texas. It started at Fort Belknap, went north along the Pecos River into New Mexico to Fort Sumner. I think they've pushed up to Cheyenne right here in Wyoming. That's about 2,000 miles. I heard they made $12,000 in gold on the first trip running cattle.'

'I see what you're getting at,' said Heggarty. 'The Chugwater valley's over a hundred miles long, they can winter stock there and move it north when they're ready. So this Colonel DeVere makes a fortune and he's done it by killing my pa.' Heggarty's face burned with anger.

After a pause Leeming said, 'I know a bit about DeVere, he fought in the war for the Rebs against us. I heard some good but most of it bad. He'd like as

177

ride his horse across a bridge of his own dead troops to save himself. He was a galvanized Yankee, you know, changed sides at the end of the war. Folk like him always have to be the biggest toad in the puddle.'

'I'm going to see him and set him straight.'

'Hold it, son,' said Leeming, pushing him back in his chair. 'You won't pin anything on him. He's as slippery as a wet fish.'

'We'll see about that. His name and where he lives are all over these papers, look here and here and here.' Heggarty pointed at the papers.

'There's your ma to think about too, simmer down,' said Leeming.

Heggarty leaned back in his chair, lost in thought for a long time.

'I'm going to see this DeVere tonight. I can get over to him and back by tomorrow. I'm going to tell him he can have the land, I want my ma back safe.'

Leeming looked startled.

'But you cain't let him win. I saw too

many good young boys killed in the war against the likes of him. We owe it to them not to let some southern scum like DeVere trample over us.'

'Winning ain't about the likes of him. For me, winning's about being with folk you care about and doing the right thing. DeVere may have money and get this land but it ain't nothing of real value to me. The land's no use now Pa's dead anyway.'

Sheriff Leeming's eyes crinkled when he smiled and said, 'Goddamn it if you ain't right.'

'But I'll tell you this for nothing, Marcello and Stanton will pay for killing my pa. I'll settle their hash once and for all. I'm going to get even, I swear I will. No one messes with my family.'

Leeming looked at him and nodded.

'You're right both ways up.'

Heggarty and Ahiga set off to find the Colonel; they rode away into the darkness where the trees on the ridge were silhouetted in the moonlight and looked like black metal crosses.

18

Marcello and Stanton arrived at Colonel DeVere's spread, unaware that Heggarty was cutting across country to the same place. It was a fine house, two-storeyed and oak-shaded with steps leading up to a double door and a first floor veranda that ran across the front of the building.

Marcello knocked on the door and they heard the noise echo inside. A lamp flared in an upstairs room. A figure leaned over the balcony rail and studied the two men and in a hushed voice said, 'Ride around the back to the stables,' and without waiting the man disappeared.

Colonel DeVere stepped out of a side door dressed immaculately in a white suit and a thin bootlace tie, a starched collar and a short-brimmed Stetson. He held his shoulders and back as straight as a parade ground officer. He looked like a pair of polished boots.

'Gentlemen,' he said, 'I can only

assume that matters of the gravest consequence bring you here uninvited at this hour. State your business.'

'Colonel,' said Marcello, 'we've just about finished the land deals around Powder River. There's one more to get done and things are set right dandy.'

'Sir,' said DeVere, 'you sorely test my patience. One more deal is not what I want to hear. One more deal means your job remains unfinished.' Marcello started to speak but DeVere held up his hand to silence him. 'Have the good manners not to interrupt me, sir. I do not want your excuses. I will pay well as you know, earn your money, sir. And you, Mr Marcello, have the good manners to dismount when you talk with me.'

Marcello climbed down off his horse and took his hat off. DeVere nodded and said, 'Thank you, now Mr Marcello, explain.'

'Well, there's a small hiccup but I'll sort it out tomorrow. The last family holding out are called Heggarty. We've killed the husband but we've got the widow and we'll make her sign. I'd like you to have my money ready tomorrow. Once I've collected my dues I aim to disappear.'

Stanton watched Marcello, he noticed it was all about Marcello and what he was going to do. Stanton smiled to himself.

'Mr Marcello, do not bore me with details or excuses,' said DeVere. 'I said I would pay when you have all of the lands that I asked for. That I will do. I suggest that you kill all of these reluctant individuals — Heggarty did you say? — or pay them off or do both. That is your job and how you do it is not my concern. That is why I engage people like you. Come back tomorrow when you have completed your task. Your money will be ready for you. Goodnight.'

Marcello mounted up and rode off around the side of the house. As Stanton put his boot in his stirrup, DeVere clasped his arm with surprising strength and whispered, 'Mr Stanton, please dispose of Marcello before your return. You may regard that as your final task. I will pay you Marcello's share, let us call it a terminal bonus. Goodnight, sir.'

'No problem,' said Stanton. 'I'd have done it for nothing.'

★ ★ ★

An hour later, Heggarty rode down out of the hills to DeVere's place. He did not know that Marcello and Stanton had just left along the main trail while he travelled through the high country. He left Ahiga in the trees.

Colonel DeVere invited him into his study.

They sat in two swayback deer hide chairs in front of the fireplace. The fire was banked up and the light flickered across their faces and the shadows shifted on the panelled walls.

DeVere's face looked like stretched rubber, his unblinking eyes like two black marbles, his thin hair combed like strands of wire across his bald head. He rested his elbows on the chair arms and steepled his fingers under his chin. A heavily muscled dog with coarse black hair lay at his feet.

'You said that you are concerned for your mother, sir, how can I help?' said DeVere. 'I believe that you said that your name is Heggarty. I'm sorry but I am unfamiliar with that name.' He lied, with a smile fixed on his face like a Hallowe'en mask.

'Maybe so,' said Heggarty, 'but you'll know Marcello and Stanton.' DeVere nodded. 'Well, they've taken my ma and they'll force her to sign over our land to you. I'm talking about land north of here around Powder River. I've seen the paperwork for the other land in your name, tell me I'm wrong.'

DeVere's mouth tightened in anger and he said, 'That is a private matter.'

'I don't give a goddamn cuss.'

The dog sensed the tension and raised his head, a string of slobber hung from the side of his mouth as his lip curled. DeVere snapped his fingers and the dog dropped his head and rested it on his paws.

'Please, Mr Heggarty, I would appreciate no more profanity in my home. Yes, I own land there and in many other areas. Yes, Marshal Marcello and Mr Stanton are my agents in these matters in and around Powder River. But I assure you that their methods are not known to me and I am not responsible for how they go about their business. I suggest that you take up any problems with those two gentlemen,' said DeVere.

'That I will,' said Heggarty. 'Look, my main problem is my ma's safety. If you want the land you can have it. But we do the deal now so that all of this ends tonight. I'll sign for her but it must be now so that I can get back and make sure that she's safe.'

DeVere wriggled with pleasure and smirked as he said, 'A wise decision, we can settle here and now. You will no doubt tell Marshal Marcello. I cannot help you as I have no contact with him.'

It took only twenty minutes for DeVere to prepare the papers, when he came back into the room two men followed and stood in silence by the doorway, their hands on the butts of their guns.

'A precaution, Mr Heggarty,' said DeVere with a mocking smile. 'Please sign.'

Heggarty signed and DeVere tossed a bundle of money onto the table and pushed it across to Heggarty with his fingertips.

'Two thousand dollars, if you care to count it,' said DeVere but Heggarty ignored him and folded the money into his jacket pocket. He walked out of the door brushing past the two men who, with a nod from DeVere, stepped aside. Heggarty paused in the doorway and put on his hat.

'Something smart to say, Mr Heggarty?' said DeVere.

Heggarty knew that DeVere was trying to goad him but he showed no emotion as he said, 'No. You run people off, kill, kidnap and threaten ordinary folk. You cheat and lie and use people just like you did in the war. I expect that's normal to you. But I'll be seeing you again, believe it.'

'I doubt that very much, sir,' said DeVere, 'my business in these parts is now over, I will be gone within the week. Do give my regards to your mother and leave the land, my land, immediately. I trust that you'll settle your differences with Marcello and Stanton one way or another.' And the door closed in Heggarty's face.

'We'll settle things right enough,' said Heggarty, his thumbs hooked in his gun belt. 'I'll salt their hides and nail them to the barn door.'

19

As Sam Heggarty sold the land, Albert and Elijah arrived back at the Heggarty place with Hannah Heggarty. Sheriff Leeming watched them in and was surprised at how happy he felt to see Hannah again.

'Hannah, am I glad to see you! What happened?'

She walked over while Elijah tied up the horses by the water trough. Leeming gave her an awkward hug. 'This is Albert and Elijah Pugh, they rescued me from Ned Stanton's cellar. Marcello and Stanton have gone, for now anyway.'

Leeming clapped Albert on the shoulder. 'Thank you kindly, sir,' he said. 'Come on in.'

Leeming watched Hannah Heggarty move around the kitchen. He sat in a comfortable chair by the fire and thought he had never been so content and at ease. Later, as they sat around the kitchen table, Leeming could eat but he watched in awe as Albert and Elijah demolished heaped plates of pork chops, biscuits, milk gravy, egg, grits and sliced tomatoes. They did not speak as they spooned the food into their mouths, cramming it in as if they had not eaten for a week. At last Albert pushed his plate away and belched.

'Fine chow, Hannah,' he said.

Elijah still had his head down over his plate, shovelling food down like there was no tomorrow.

Leeming packed two pipes and handed one to Albert who lit it and inhaled, holding the smoke down in his lungs before blowing out a grey plume that wreathed his head and face.

'Obliged,' said Albert.

Leeming looked at Hannah Heggarty and his eyes shone with concern as he explained what they had found out and where Sam was. He said, 'Sam's likely sold the land.'

'It doesn't matter,' said Hannah Heggarty. 'I can't keep this place up now on my own. I just want my boy back safe.'

Leeming nodded and said, 'That's just about what Sam thought, but we need to tell him you're safe. Stanton and Marcello can't threaten him now. He needs to know that you've got away in case he runs into them. Selling the land means he can deal with Stanton and Marcello, nothing's going to stop him doing that.'

'I'll go and meet him,' said Elijah. 'I can wait for him and tell him we got his ma out and she's home safe.'

'I'd best stay here,' said Albert through a hacking cough. 'Stanton and Marcello will be high tailing it over here once they see Hannah's gone. Listen good, Elijah, don't you go sticking your head down no porcupine hole, you don't go looking for trouble. You just ride out and wait for Hannah's boy.'

'I'm not sure which way he'll be coming back in,' said Leeming. 'He has a Shoshone guide and they might not use the main trail.'

'I can wait for him out there a piece,' said Elijah, pointing over his shoulder.

'All the trails come out down by Cripple Bend, right, Pa?'

'They do. You look out for that boy and for yourself, Elijah,' said Albert.

'Don't you worry any about me, Pa,' said Elijah, holding his plate up and licking it clean.

Later, in the blue glow of the early dawn, Elijah Pugh cantered out across country to meet Heggarty. He rode for half an hour then walked his horse up a long gradient to a plateau where three enormous slabs of rock lay, one on top of another. He climbed them and sat on the top with his legs hanging in space and watched the buzzards turning in the sky; the wind pushed his coat open and pulled at his hat brim.

He waited until he saw two shadowy figures loom out of the mist along the main trail, their silhouettes drifting in and out of sight in the cloudbank that swirled along the foot of the hillside.

Elijah stood, waved his hat and hollered, 'Heggarty, over here, we've got your ma safe.'

He saw the two riders stop and look up. Elijah scrambled down the rocks, jumped on his mule, cracked the palm of his hand across its rump and rode full tilt to meet them. The sun broke across the ridge and the mist and shadows lifted immediately as Elijah hunched down close to the mule's shoulder and thundered to his fate.

'Who in hell's that?' said Stanton, squinting against the glare.

'We'll find out right soon,' said Marcello, levering a round into the breech of his Winchester and slowing his horse with his fat thighs.

Fifty yards away, Elijah glanced up and the smile froze on his face as he recognized Marcello and Stanton.

'It's Elijah Pugh,' said Marcello.

He raised the rifle and fired, his shot grazing a rock behind Elijah's mule. His second shot glanced off the mule's withers and it stumbled and pitched forward on its shoulder, throwing Elijah into the air. He crashed into a rock with a sickening thud but managed to roll behind it.

They saw him pull his gun as he ducked out of sight.

Elijah fired two wild shots and Marcello and Stanton wheeled away in opposite directions. Elijah rolled onto his back and patted his pockets for spare cartridges. He felt three bullets in his trousers and knew that was as good as it was going to get. He had six bullets in all. He put the hammer on half-cock and shucked out the empty shell casings on the floor, rotated the cylinder and inserted the fresh rounds. He turned back over onto his front and pain flared low in his back where he crashed into the rocks. His right leg was numb and he knew then he wasn't going anywhere.

He saw movement away to his left and he fired, the gun bucked in his hand three times as he pulled the trigger and hoped for the best. He heard one bullet thunk into wood and another splinter a rock and prayed he had hit Marcello. He jumped when he heard a boot scrape on shale behind him and he swung and fired at the sound until the hammer clicked on an empty chamber.

A shadow fell across his face and he heard Stanton say, 'It's over, Pugh.'

Stanton raised his right hand Smith and Wesson and casually shot Elijah in the left leg, the bullet exited in a gush of blood. Elijah glanced down at his bloody leg, amazed at the lack of pain. He threw his empty gun at Stanton and it bounced off his chest and clattered onto the rocks.

Marcello walked across and looked down at Elijah with contempt.

'You weren't even close, Pugh,' he said. 'Where's your no good pa got to?'

'He's waiting to kill the two of you,' said Elijah with a dry cough, his mouth felt like it was clogged with ash. 'What did you shout about Mrs Heggarty?' said Stanton, kicking Elijah's foot.

Elijah smiled. 'She's safe, mister, we found her in the cellar. I wouldn't like to be in your shoes now, you've got yourself a whole mess of trouble.'

'Where is she?' snapped Marcello and he raised his gun and snapped a shot off, hitting Elijah in the chest. Elijah's body jerked but he stared at Marcello and smiled, he tried to speak but his voice caught in his throat. Marcello stepped over, bent down and put his face close to Elijah's head.

'Come on, boy,' he said, 'make it easy on yourself.'

Elijah blinked, he worked his jaw until his mouth felt warm and moist and he spat a gob of phlegm clotted with blood into Marcello's face. Marcello jerked back in disgust, his cheek strung with gore. Elijah grinned, showing his bloodstained teeth and gums, he looked off into the sunlight and finally said, 'She's back home with the sheriff and my pa, you skunk. And the next bullet that hits you will tear out your goddamn black heart.'

As he spoke a great tiredness seeped through his body. He felt heavy and warm as if he had his pa's hand on his chest, pressing him down into the earth. He laid his head back against the rocks and thought dying wasn't so bad after all. He stopped breathing.

'Come on,' said Stanton to Marcello,

his eyes as savage as a meat axe. 'Let's burn the breeze. It's time to face them down and see who walks away.'

★ ★ ★

An hour later, Heggarty and Ahiga came down off the mountains and the peaks looked as sharp as jagged teeth against the horizon. They rode with the sunrise behind them, a flood of warm air and light spread out in front of them, lifting the trees and rocks out of the shadows.

'There,' said Ahiga, pointing at three buzzards circling in the air; drifting like ash off a fire, they dropped and melted into the rocks.

'We'll take a look,' said Heggarty and they cantered down the gradient towards the main trail.

Ahiga held up his hand and Heggarty pulled in behind him as Ahiga nodded down towards the hoof prints outlined in the trail dust. He slid from his saddle and studied the horse droppings littering the tracks.

196

'They pass maybe one hour ago. Two men, the marshal and gunman.' He looked up at Heggarty, his lean face smooth and tan like parchment in the morning light.

Heggarty frowned and said, 'I bet they've been up to see that dadburn Colonel. That means he lied to my face. I'll settle with him by God once this is over. The land's not important but he'll pay in blood for the mess of grief he put on my family.' He looked at Ahiga and could see that most of what he said was lost on him. 'Thank you, Ahiga, for your help. Let's check what the buzzards are feeding on.'

They spooked the buzzards and saw them lift into the air, their large wings slapping like leather as they pulled themselves up and away from their meal.

Ahiga grunted as he looked across the scree and they saw Elijah's body splayed on the ground, the air thick with insects. The grass and rocks were stippled with blood that had pooled and dried on the dirt in reddish patches.

'It's Elijah Pugh,' said Heggarty, noticing the bullet wounds. 'They played with him first.'

He looked up at the sky, his jaw rigid with anger and his face flat and brutal. He looked back down at Elijah.

'Don't you worry, mister, I'll square this for you.'

20

Sheriff Leeming, Albert Pugh and Hannah Heggarty expected trouble and prepared to defend themselves. 'Listen good,' said Leeming. 'I reckon Stanton and Marcello will be coming in hard today once they see Hannah's gone. They'll be loaded for bear and mean as hell. We need to hold them off until Sam gets back. We stay in the cabin and prepare for war. Albert, you take the back window, hunker down and shoot anything that moves.' Albert nodded, chewing on a plug of Leeming's tobacco. 'We'll bar the other windows and the door, I'll take a front window.'

They looked down at the guns on the kitchen table. Albert had an old Sharps 50 rifle and a Colt New Army model 1860 revolver from before the war.

Leeming frowned at them. 'That Sharps is single shot action, so you've to slow reload every time.'

'I do,' said Albert, brushing his fingers across the walnut grip, 'and paper cartridges. But I'm used to it and I like it right fine. This here is a Slant Breech as good as new, I can shoot the nuts of a bull at 700 yards.'

'Well, take a Henry rifle as well, will you? Hannah has one you can use. They hold sixteen rounds. They used to say that you could load on Sunday and shoot all week long. Here, take a couple of boxes of cartridges with you.'

Albert coughed and his breath crackled in his lungs as if they were made from rotted cork.

'I'll load for you, Albert, if you need me. That's my husband's rifle, I know it well,' said Hannah Heggarty.

Sheriff Leeming leaned his own rifle against the wall, turned and looked at her.

'Hannah, I'll tip the table and you get behind it when the trouble kicks in. Keep the shotgun, if we holler you help me or Albert when we need you, is that all right with you?'

'That I will do, Lewis,' said Hannah. She took two shotgun shells out of the box, broke the gun and slotted them into the barrels with an oily clack and snapped the breech shut. She tied her hair back, winked at Albert and the two of them went around the cabin barring the windows.

'We're gonna have us a real hog killing time,' said Albert, his jaw packed with tobacco, his breath whistling like wind in a clogged chimney.

'Leeming,' shouted Marcello outside.

'Goddamn it, they're here already,' muttered Leeming as he levered a round into his Remington and peeked around the edge of the window frame.

'Leeming,' repeated Marcello, 'give it up. We've got no beef with you. Back down now, there's no need for any more blood spilling.' No-one believed him. 'I've checked the stable and yard, we know it's just you and that ornery old coot Pugh.' He paused and lifted his voice. 'Albert, your no good boy is dead, if you don't want to join him, get out here now.'

Mrs Heggarty pushed her hair back off her face with the back of her wrist and walked into the other room to find Albert. She saw him by the window with his shoulders hunched and his head bent forward on his chest.

'I'm sorry, Albert,' she whispered.

'Maybe he's lying.' Albert spoke to her without turning and then he swung his head towards her. He closed and opened his eyes to blink away the tears and his voice caught in his throat. 'He was a good boy, he didn't deserve that if it's right.'

He busied himself with his guns, picked up the Henry rifle and fiddled with the stock absent-mindedly.

He saw movement at the back of the barn, a shadow moved and the spangled sunlight caught a glint of gun metal. Albert's face filled with anger, his temper sharper than a stropped razor. He whipped the rifle to his shoulder and fired into the trees. The room filled with noise and gun smoke as Albert triggered the rifle, levering bullets into the breech as quickly as he could. They whined through the air, shredding leaves and snapping branches until the rifle clicked empty. Albert tossed it aside and picked up his old Sharps. He spat on his hand and slapped it onto the rifle stock for luck then rested the barrel across the window sill and, beyond caring, stood silhouetted in the window.

Stanton hid at the back of the barn and when Albert first opened up, he threw himself to the ground. He lay flat in the undergrowth as Albert's shots showered him in leaves and dust. When the firing stopped and the echoes faded, Stanton lifted his head and called, 'You need to do better than that, mister,' so that Albert could get a fix on where he lay. Then he crawled backwards a few yards, rolled into a ditch and moved away to his right. He slithered through a clump of low bushes and bellied up to the top of a small rise. He took his hat off and peeped over the top, tucked the rifle stock into his shoulder and sighted down the barrel.

Albert stood in the window and fired using a single shot rifle but reloading with impressive speed, he shot into the bushes where Stanton had called from a moment ago. He watched the big recoil lift the barrel after each shot and the smoke drift up into the air.

Stanton drew a bead on Albert's chest, squeezed the trigger and saw Albert's jacket puff with dust as he hit him high in the upper body. Albert staggered back and fell from sight. Stanton smiled.

Albert's eyes followed Hannah Heggarty as she moved across the room and he gave a weak smile before his head fell on his chest. Hannah picked up the Henry rifle, reloaded it and sprayed a handful of bullets into the trees behind the cabin. In a soft voice, she called across the cabin.

'Lewis, I'm afraid Albert's been hit.'

'Is he dead?'

'No, but he's hit bad.'

'Can you cover back there, Hannah?' said Leeming. 'You bet,' said Hannah. Leeming smiled to himself. He heard two

204

shots out front and saw them gouge wood out of the corner of the barn and heard Sam Heggarty call, 'Stay down, Sheriff, I'll fix Marcello.' Another shot thudded against the barn wall, forcin Marcello to break cover. He waddled down the front of the barn, threw himself through the open doorway and rolled into the shadows inside. He moved like a bale of hay.

Heggarty raced across the yard, he fired his gun from the hip as he ran to the barn door. He flattened himself against the front wall to reload, checked a second revolver, shoved it down the front of his trousers and ran into the barn.

21

He stepped into the small dark barn with slim columns of sunlight poking through the walls and warm air smelling of horse. He blinked in the poor light, half in and half out of the door. They both fired at the same time. The flash from the guns filled the barn in a blinding light. Heggarty was unhurt but knew he had missed Marcello. He jacked the trigger five more times, pumping bullets in Marcello's direction and dived forward, following his bullets deeper into the building.

He rolled behind the wooden slats of the first stall, pulled a handful of bullets from his pocket and thumbed them into the cylinder just as the stall wall shredded as Marcello blasted away with his gun. Splinters showered Heggarty's face but he ignored them and fired three fast shots at the gun flash and he heard Marcello gasp in pain and disappear in the gloom by the far wall. Smoke swirled and hung in the air, the smell burning his throat. Then Heggarty caught sight of Marcello, his body like a tree stump crouched down by a pile of straw. Heggarty lifted his Smith and Wesson two-handed and fired two shots and rolled away into the dark as a shot walloped into the wood where he had just been, telling him that Marcello was still alive.

Marcello was terribly afraid, he shrank back into the corner; his breath came in wracking sobs and his thick body trembled with pain and fear. Heggarty fired again, a cloud of dust showered down on him, he ducked and felt a searing pain in his arm. He turned towards the shot and saw Heggarty behind a stall. Marcello's eyes filled with an insane light and he began to fire, his left arm hung at his side, soaked in blood. He pulled the trigger again but nothing happened so he simply started to walk towards Heggarty, clicking an empty gun.

Heggarty reloaded and kept firing, aiming at Marcello's thick body but still he came on. The bullets thumped home and it felt to Heggarty like he was shooting into a sack of grain. Heggarty's hand tingled, his mouth was dry and his hair damp with sweat. Marcello staggered and toppled to his knees but he gritted his teeth and climbed back to his feet. Heggarty fired again, the gun bucked in his tired hand and he struggled to bring it back into line.

Marcello threw himself on top of Heggarty, pressing down with his huge weight, his blood slick and sticky on his hands and face. Marcello's big hardened hands closed on Heggarty's throat as Heggarty tried to squirm out from under him. Heggarty remembered his other gun, he worked it out from the waistband of his trousers, stuck it under Marcello's armpit and squeezed the trigger twice and Marcello slumped against him.

Heggarty rolled him off and lay for a moment with his eyes closed then pulled himself to his feet using a stall for support.

Outside, Ahiga listened to the shooting in the barn. He walked behind the cabin. He held his brother's bow and two arrows against the length of the bow shaft. He crawled through the under-growth, pushed into coarse grass and saw Stanton laid beneath him on a low ridge. Stanton watched the back window down his rifle barrel, the stock tight to his shoulder. Ahiga knelt, stuck one of his arrows in the soft soil by his knee, notched the other and drew the gut string back into his cheek with his fingers.

Heggarty shouted, 'Marcello's dead,' and the barn door creaked open.

Stanton swung his rifle sideways and aimed across the yard to the barn. Ahiga had no choice but to rush his shot. He snapped his fingers away from the string and the arrow whooshed down the slope at Stanton. The arrow grazed Stanton's head and buried itself in the ground in front of him. Stanton cursed and his hand went to the side of his head where the arrow sliced his ear. He rolled away and slid out of sight. Ahiga heard him crashing through the undergrowth and a moment later, heard a horse ride away. He ran to the top of the hill and watched Stanton crouched on his big roan, galloping off into the distance. Ahiga turned and saw Heggarty standing in the yard looking up at him.

'He's gone,' Ahiga called. 'I bring horses in,' and he loped off through the trees.

★   ★   ★

Stanton raced down the valley, his horse's neck and flanks dark with sweat, its mouth strung with wisps of saliva.

He stomped into the bedroom at his cabin, his footsteps echoed on the rough timber floor in the stale hot air. The room stood empty and joyless as though it had not seen anything worth remembering. He did not feel like he belonged anywhere.

He filled his saddle bag with everything he owned — about $200, his gun cleaning gear, ammunition, a curry comb, a brush and a picket pin to stake out the horse. He found a long sleeved black shirt and an old pair of brown trousers. He tightened the leather straps and buckled the half full pouches. He picked up his duster and rolled the coat inside his bedroll then he crossed to the door and walked out without looking back, the door slammed behind him, a hollow echo ran through the house like a lament.

He stood, rested his arms across the horse's withers and looked across the valley for a long time, listening. He touched his wounded ear with the tips of his fingers and looked at the blood. The cut was drying but stung like hell, rough-edged like jagged tin. A goddamn Indian working with Heggarty, he thought, and in another minute, he would have nailed Heggarty as he stepped out of the barn. He wished he had time to pay Heggarty back for the beating. He smiled to himself, thinking about killing Heggarty's mother first and then Heggarty face to face and gun to gun.

He ground his teeth in frustration,

tomorrow was another day and he would meet it head on with his gun in his hand. He shouted, 'There'll be a reckoning. I'll make your lives a living hell.' His voice rolled like thunder across the yard, through scattered small holdings, clumps of trees and rocks, railed hog pens and empty pasture on towards Powder River.

★ ★ ★

As Stanton ran off, Leeming pushed open the cabin door and limped outside, holding his rifle across his chest.

'Is my ma all right?' Heggarty asked.

'She's fine and dandy, son. She's quite a gal, ain't she?' said Leeming and smiled for a moment before his face hardened. 'Albert's hit bad. Is it right about Elijah?'

'Yes, it's true, they took him down hard. We found him on the way back and brought him in,' said Heggarty.

Mrs Heggarty hurried out of the cabin, ran to her son and hugged him, burying her head in his shoulder.

212

'Albert's dead,' she said in a soft voice. 'That's your pa, Albert and Elijah all gone. Stanton and Marcello are such evil men.'

Leeming walked across and laid his hand on her shoulder.

'Hannah, we'll bury Albert and Elijah next to the creek with your permission, they did right by us. Trouble always brings out the best in decent folk.' He looked at Heggarty. 'Did you sell the land?'

'Yes, I did. I met this Colonel DeVere. He lied to me about Stanton and Marcello, he's in it with them of course. In fact, it's his show. But he was happy to get the land. He thinks it's all over but I ain't finished yet.'

'So they all died for nothing in the end, he got the land anyway,' said Mrs Heggarty.

'They all stood up for what they believed in at least. Fine men that shame the likes of Marcello and Stanton. And there's still some dying to do, I'm going after Stanton,' said Heggarty.

'Come,' said Ahiga, 'time to ride.'

Heggarty turned to Leeming.

'Will you take my ma into town, she'll be safer there.'

'I will, son, don't you fret about it, you've enough on your plate,' said Leeming, resting a hand on Hannah's shoulder again.

'I'll come by tomorrow, hopefully,' said Heggarty. He drew a gun, opened the loading gate, pulled back the hammer and rotated the cylinder, watching the chambers click through one at a time before reloading it from his cartridge belt and sliding it back into his rig.

Mrs Heggarty frowned as she watched him load his other gun; red-eyed, she stared at him with her lips pressed together, too upset to talk. Leeming tried to comfort her, saying, 'Listen, when we get to Powder River, I'll get word to the Federal Marshals in Owl Creek. I'll tell them about Marcello and square things off so that we can get some new lawmen in place.'

'Be safe, Sam,' said Mrs Heggarty, looking at her son with fondness.

'Don't worry, Ma,' said Heggarty. 'I'll get this settled with Stanton, that I promise you. Ahiga will track him and I'll take him out. He ain't worth a glass of hot gravy in July.'

Mrs Heggarty bit at her bottom lip but Leeming laughed and said, 'Go in hard, shoot straight and put him down good.' He looked across at Hannah. 'Your boy's someone to ride the river with, Hannah, don't you concern yourself about him.'

They watched Heggarty move up the slope, he had a quiet way of walking, as sinewy as a cougar he seemed to glide across the ground like the big cat's shadow.

Leeming turned to Mrs Heggarty and said, 'You'll be safe in town, Hannah, it's the last place Stanton will be heading for.'

22

When they arrived in Powder River, Sheriff Leeming went to check Marcello's room. He worried about Sam Heggarty, he knew Stanton was a dangerous man because he knew his type, dirty white crackers who thought nothing of killing, mean unhappy men with a fast gun and a heart carved out of stone.

As he unlocked the door, he did not hear the boot scuff the boards inside the room. Unfortunately he did not notice the shadow that flickered across the threshold under the door. He pushed the door open and looked at the ransacked room. The bed was upended and clothes littered the floor, the curtain by the open window billowed in the breeze and pushed the smell of tobacco and stale sweat into his face. As Leeming moved further into the room, Stanton came out from behind the door and clubbed him on the back of the head with his gun butt. Leeming went down like a sack of horse shoes. When he came round, he felt warm blood trickle out of his hairline and down his neck, his head pounded from the blow. He struggled to push himself up and managed to get onto his hands and knees.

'Sheriff Leeming as I recall,' said Stanton from behind him.

Leeming coughed and spoke without turning.

'Do what you've got to do, Stanton, go on shoot, goddamn it. I won't make it easy for you.'

Stanton laughed.

'Oh ain't you a tough old hillbilly, mister. I'll shoot you no matter what, it's just a question of when and I'll decide that. It looks like you're riding solo today, partner, so I'll just take my own sweet time. Maybe let you think about dying, let the fear gnaw at your belly before I finish you. You owe me, you know, you and that Heggarty are a mite tiresome. But for what? You've gone and got yourself killed for $200 a month, lying there in an all-fired mess for next to nothing. At least as a lawman Marcello had the right idea, he thought he could make good money on the side and get out. He almost did it too.'

Leeming looked back over his shoulder and smiled. 'Almost doesn't make it though, does it? Sometimes you get and sometimes you get got. Marcello's dead. Heggarty will find you and take you down whatever happens to me. Your money ain't worth spit.'

He turned away from Stanton to hide his pain, he felt as though someone had pulled him through a bucket of broken glass. 'There's no reason to kill Mrs Heggarty now, the land's been sold.'

Stanton scowled, his right eye still swollen, it looked like a split plum.

'Old man, I don't need a reason to kill her or her son. I don't do this for money. I like killing. Now as it happens Marcello did have upwards of $800, I found his stash just before you blundered in. I'll keep that. But you see, Marcello's dead and you, well, you're going to die too but me, why I'll ride on out of it and live to kill another day. I know who I'd rather be.'

Leeming said, 'You'll be dead within a week, Heggarty will see to that. Folk like you are always running. He whupped you good and you're scared of him.'

He heard a match strike and he smelt smoke as Stanton lit a cigarette, he saw the smoke drift to the open window and hang in the air.

'See, you don't get it, Leeming, do you?' said Stanton. 'I know I'll die someday. I don't care. It's like a game of Faro, I always bet to win. I'm still in the game but if it goes belly up and I die, well, I'll go out smiling.'

Leeming heard Stanton cock his gun, pull the hammer back.

'That's a fine sound, ain't it?' Stanton stepped across the room and Leeming felt the cold hard barrel press against the back of his head.

'You just lost, old man,' said Stanton as his finger tightened on the trigger.

Leeming lashed out backwards with

his wooden leg and caught Stanton on the shin. Stanton felt as if someone had whacked him with a hammer and he stumbled and half spun around. Leeming pushed himself up, lurched for the window and threw himself forward, Stanton fired at his back and the bullet struck Leeming and pushed him out of the window in an explosion of glass and noise.

Heggarty entered the main street heading towards the store. He dismounted and stood holding his horse by the bridle and bit when he heard a shot. Above him, a window shattered and a figure crashed out, rolled down the boardwalk roof and hit the ground with a thud in a cloud of dust.

Heggarty started towards the body when he saw Leeming push himself up on one elbow and shout, 'It's Stanton, forget about me and get after him. It's now, Sam, it's your time, get it done.'

Heggarty heard a thump on the roof of the boardwalk and the hollow sound of someone running across the boards. He followed the noise with his eyes towards the end of the building and saw Stanton jump down at the corner and disappear into the shadows of an alleyway.

On the slope above town, Ahiga saw Stanton's horse tied to a post at the back of a building. He notched an arrow to his brother's bow and walked down the shoulder of the hill. Stanton rushed out from between two buildings and started towards his horse. Ahiga drew the bow and shot for the post where the horse was hitched. The arrow thunked into the wood and the startled horse reared its head and pawed at the dusty ground, pulling on the reins. Stanton skidded to a halt, saw the Shoshone draw his bow for the second time and he turned and ran back into the alley-way.

'Stanton,' said a voice that Stanton recognized straightaway and he spun to his right.

Heggarty stood at the far end of the alley, his feet slightly apart. He hitched his belt up as the gun rig pulled down on his hips. Stanton rolled his shoulders and stretched his fingers.

'Heggarty,' said Stanton, his voice deep and raspy. 'First off, you got here too late to save your pa and now that old dog, the sheriff. I reckon you'll be late for your own funeral. Come on, let's find out.'

'Drop the gun, Stanton, it's over,' said Heggarty. 'Don't make me do what I'm thinking.'

There was a long still silence, the air hung heavy and hot and Heggarty felt a single bead of sweat trickle down his back.

Stanton said, 'Let's settle this like real men. You're not scared of me, are you?'

'I'm trying to be, Stanton, but I guess your tough man act doesn't work on me,' said Heggarty in a quiet voice. His eyes locked on Stanton. 'Come on then, let's get to it.'

'When you're ready,' said Stanton, his face filled with arrogance and cruelty. Confident and relaxed, he waited with dark, deep, empty eyes; he looked as mean as death, his scowling face pale and bitter.

Heggarty made the first move and went for his gun. Stanton was astonished at how fast Heggarty moved his arm, it seemed like a blurred flash but instinctively his own hand dropped and drew and he fired as soon as the gun cleared the rig. Stanton knew he made the first shot as the gun kicked in his hand and he fanned the hammer with the palm of his hand and fired again.

His first shot should have taken Heggarty in the chest or throat but in one fluid movement as Heggarty went for his gun, he dropped to one knee. Stanton's first bullet flew over him, crossed the street and shattered a window. Stanton's second wild gunshot slammed into the saloon wall. Heggarty ignored both blasts, held his gun two-handed, sighted down the barrel and with the front sight square on Stanton's chest, he squeezed the trigger. He watched the bullet punch into Stanton's body, knock him back a step and make him grunt in pain and shock.

Heggarty's second bullet hit Stanton in the groin and he went down hard. He lay on his back, his chest heaved as he fought for air, his breathing ragged and wet as blood filled his mouth and clogged his lungs. He tried to sit but his blood and strength drained into the hot dirt of the alley, it felt as though his chest was wrapped in chains. He opened his eyes as a shadow fell across his face and he looked up to see Heggarty stood over him.

'It's not all about speed, Stanton,' said Heggarty, 'you got to hit the other feller as well. Sure and right gets it done.'

Stanton coughed blood, he worked his mouth and whispered, 'I don't regret none of it. If I had to do it again I'd do it exactly the same way. I never expected anything from life and never got nothing either.'

'You deserved what you got from me, I paid out my justice in bullets,' said Heggarty.

Stanton nodded but could not smile, he shuddered and died.

Ahiga walked up to Heggarty and said, 'It's over.' Heggarty looked up at him and said, 'Not yet.'

23

At dawn the next day the hidden sharp-shooter loaded his rifle and waited, he knew that he had one shot and it must be a killing shot.

Hannah Heggarty was leaving today to move in with her son Sam and his family. She made arrangements for her furniture to be moved on to her and for the livestock to be sold off. One way or another, her time in Powder River was over.

Sheriff Lewis Leeming decided to resign as a County Sheriff, his leg bothered him and the recent shoulder wound needed to heal. He knew it was time to get out while he could. It was his last day in Powder River but he hoped to see more of Hannah Heggarty, whatever else the future held. Colonel Lovell DeVere also planned to leave today. He sold the whole of his land holdings to the major cattle businesses in Cheyenne. He wanted to establish the Texas Longhorn across Wyoming. He did not know what his future held but thought today was a good place for it to start.

Ahiga's time in Powder River was over. He headed north towards the Owl Creek Mountains and the Shoshone Reservation. He felt that he rode with his brother, believing that he was not dead while he lived in his own heart.

★ ★ ★

They did not know that the sharp-shooter waited or who he waited for. He found a place for himself in the rocks at the last climb that led up to the valley. He sat in absolute silence and stillness, his back against a slab of rock, cradling the heavy rifle across his knees.

When his target appeared, he stayed calm even after his long wait. He did not get excited, did not move, he simply concentrated on the kill.

He hid over 600 yards away and knew that he was well hidden.

As he watched, the man turned and looked up in his direction. He knew that the man could not see him but he seemed to feel his gaze wash over him and it felt like their eyes met, but he knew that he imagined it.

Sam Heggarty stood and carefully lifted the rifle. He slid it up, smooth and sure, without thinking about it. A movement he had made thousands of times before, through years of practice. He drew the rifle to his shoulder, rested his elbows on the rock in front of him, adjusted his shoulders and locked his arms in place.

He rested his cheek on to the rifle stock and felt the warm, smooth wood against his face like a caress. He looked down the barrel.

He knew that when he squeezed the trigger, the gun would jolt into his shoulder but he was ready for it and prepared for the shot. He cocked the hammer and curled his finger around the trigger.

Colonel DeVere sat alone on the first

floor balcony of his house and ate a fine breakfast. He sipped his coffee then put the cup back on the table, tilted his head back and closed his eyes to enjoy the early sun on his face.

Heggarty squeezed the trigger and the heavy bullet tore off the mountain, across the plain and smashed into DeVere. The impact slammed him against the wall and shattered his chest. His face and forehead veined with blood and coffee. Dead.

Heggarty took his time walking back down to his horse. He held the rifle stock in his right hand and the barrel rested on his shoulder, it was Albert Pugh's Sharps 50 rifle.

'I think you'd have been right proud of that shot, Albert, my pa sure did teach me how to shoot well.' He smiled to himself. He mounted up and rode off. It was his last day in Powder River, he would take his ma home with him.

He felt certain that no one would link him to DeVere's death, after all, he had sold the land to him and their business was done.

Well, everything was settled between them now.

We do hope that you have enjoyed reading this large print book.

Did you know that all of our titles are available for purchase?

We publish a wide range of high quality large print books including:
Romances, Mysteries, Classics General Fiction Non Fiction and Westerns

Special interest titles available in large print are:
The Little Oxford Dictionary Music Book, Song Book Hymn Book, Service Book

Also available from us courtesy of Oxford University Press:
Young Readers' Dictionary (large print edition) Young Readers' Thesaurus (large print edition)

For further information or a free brochure, please contact us at:
Ulverscroft Large Print Books Ltd., The Green, Bradgate Road, Anstey, Leicester, LE7 7FU, England. Tel: (00 44) **0116 236 4325 Fax:** (00 44) **0116 234 0205**

Other titles in the
Linford Western Library:

BOUNTY BY CHANCE

J. L. Guin

Jeremiah Hackett is a young man searching for a future. On his quest, he teams up with huckster George Finimin, a tonic salesman. When Finimin is murdered, Jeremiah dedicates himself to finding the killer. But things do not prove straightforward for Jeremiah, and he needs to mature and learn some harsh lessons before he can finally achieve his aim.

WHERE NO RAVENS FLY

Harry Jay Thorn

Sometime Pinkerton Agent, Deputy US Marshal and freelance detective Lucas Santana is ordered south to Riverton County, Texas, to investigate the rumoured growing unrest there. The ambitious Frank Vagg controls the local law on both the Mexican and Texas side of the Rio Grande. When the lead begins to fly, Santana is joined by fellow Pinkerton agents Joshua Beafort and Jacob Benbow and the body count grows in the grim, grey borderline county where no ravens fly.

QUIGLEY'S WAY

P. McCormac

A dying man named Peter Barker asks Sheriff Quigley to deliver a message to his family. Quigley does so — only to find himself the target of range baron Huston McRae, who controls everything in Gila County, including the law. McRae doesn't want an outsider nosing around in his affairs, and especially not helping Peter's widow. When McRae's attempts at intimidation fail, he orders Quigley killed. But Quigley sends for his deputy, Murray Fishbourne, and together they'll take on McRae and his gunslingers.